The Riviera Affair

A Yellow Cottage Vintage Mystery Book 4

J. NEW

Cover Illustration — *William Webb*

Typography — *Coverkicks*

Copyright © 2018

ALL RIGHTS RESERVED

The use of any part of this publication reproduced, transmitted in any form or by any means, electronic, mechanical, photocopying, recording or otherwise stored in a retrieval system, without the express written consent of the author, is an infringement of the copyright law and is strictly prohibited.

This book is a work of fiction. Names, characters, places and incidents are products of the author's imagination or are used fictitiously. Any resemblance to actual events or locales or persons, living or dead is coincidental.

www.jnewwrites.com

Table of Contents

Chapter ONE 4

Chapter TWO 14

Chapter THREE 26

Chapter FOUR 44

Chapter FIVE 59

Chapter SIX 78

Chapter SEVEN 91

Chapter EIGHT 108

Chapter NINE 134

Chapter TEN 156

Chapter ELEVEN 168

Chapter TWELVE 189

Chapter THIRTEEN 199

Chapter FOURTEEN 214

Chapter FIFTEEN 232

   Other books in the series: 249

   About the Author 253

Chapter ONE

MY MOTHER HAD NEVER BEEN one to break down in the face of adversity. To me she always seemed to have an unflappable resolve to make the best of any situation and move on accordingly. So it was with some alarm that I registered the strain in her voice when she telephoned from France to ask for my help. Apparently she was about to be arrested.

"Arrested? Mother, whatever have you done?"

"Absolutely nothing, it's all just a terrible misunderstanding, Ella. You see my friend Colonel Summerfield has gone missing and Perret the detective in charge seems to think I have something to do with it. I haven't of course, but he's terribly bullish and quite sinister and I can't seem to make him listen."

"But why does he think you're involved?"

"Because I reported Edward missing and was the last person to see him before he vanished. Of course that means nothing but my concern is if Perret is focusing on me then he's not looking for the real reason Edward has disappeared."

"I assume this is unusual behaviour for the Colonel? He's not just gone away for a few days and forgotten to tell you?"

"No it's not like him at all, Ella. If he had something planned then he would have told me. It's been two days now and I'm really quite worried about him. Do you think you can come and help?"

"Yes of course, I'll be there as soon as I can."

"Thank you, darling, it will be lovely to see you even under these worrying circumstances."

"One other thing, Mother, have you told Detective Perret what my occupation is?"

There was no response and a click on the line told me our connection had been lost. I decided not to waste time trying to put another call through, I had no idea how long it would take me to get to France and from what mother had intimated speed was of the essence. I did put a call through to my aunt however, as my mother's sister it was only right I kept her informed. I also had a sneaking suspicion that once she knew the nature of my call she would insist on accompanying me.

"Elspeth arrested? I've never heard anything so preposterous in my life," Aunt Margaret said when I had told her the news. "What is this Perret's reasoning did Elspeth say?"

"Only that she was the one to report the colonel missing and was the last to see him."

"Well, he obviously doesn't have a shred of evidence and is just grasping at straws."

These were my thoughts too but it wouldn't be the first time a person had been arrested in error, and given the fact my mother was a foreigner and practically alone in a strange country, as well as having limited knowledge of the criminal laws and procedures, I was becoming increasingly anxious.

"So what happened exactly, Ella? Where were they when the colonel vanished?"

"I don't know, Aunt Margaret, I'm afraid we were cut off before I had chance to question her in detail. But she sounded worried, and not just for the colonel. I need to get there as soon as possible."

"Well, you're not going alone, dear, I shall accompany you. And what's more I think Pierre should come too, he'll be extremely valuable should things become difficult."

Pierre DuPont was a dear friend of my aunt's whom I had met on my previous case. An internationally renowned artist, I had originally thought him to be French until he lapsed into a Cockney accent. I was then informed he was indeed originally a Londoner and a master forger to boot. He was an exceptional mimic and would have been at home on either the stage or announcing the news on the wireless. He was also a dwarf and delightfully eccentric in his dress. But one thing he was not was French.

"Do you think so, aunt? He's not actually French and although I certainly couldn't tell the difference, I'm sure the people of France would recognise an interloper when they heard one."

My aunt chuckled. "You'd be surprised, Ella. Pierre lived in France for a number of years, in fact he studied at the École des Beaux-Arts, one of the most influential art schools in Paris, and by the time he left there was hardly a soul who realised he wasn't a native."

"Why am I not surprised? Well I'd be very glad to have him along in that case, I'm already feeling out of my depth and I haven't even left home yet."

"Don't worry, darling, as your mother said it's probably all just a silly misunderstanding. We'll get to the bottom of the mystery soon enough I'm sure. In fact I wouldn't be at all surprised if the colonel is already back and enjoying a cocktail on the terrace as we speak. Now you do have a passport, don't you?"

"Yes," I said, trying to remember where I had put it when I'd moved to my cottage on Linhay Island several months ago.

"Jolly good. Well, leave all the arrangements to me. I'll telephone you shortly with instructions. I expect they will send a chauffeur to pick you up from Waterloo; it's all part of the service."

I smiled, grateful the logistics of travel would be made by someone else, for I'd never travelled abroad and it would have taken me far longer. Replacing the telephone receiver on its cradle, I had only managed to take one step away when it rang again.

"Hello?"

"Hello, Ella."

It was my brother.

"Jerry, what a lovely surprise, how are you? How was your trip to Scotland? How is Ginny?"

"Goodness, let a chap take a breath, Ella," Jerry replied, laughing. "Scotland was terrific and the castle was absolutely splendid, a writer's dream in fact. I've filled a couple of notebooks with ideas for the next book and can't wait to get started."

"That's wonderful news, Jerry, but I hope you didn't leave Ginny alone too much? I know she wasn't feeling terribly well when you went to Scotland. How is she now?"

"Actually she's resting at the moment, still quite green around the gills but..."

"Have you taken her to the doctor? She really must see someone you know, this has been going on for far too long."

"Well that's why I'm calling..."

"Oh, Jerry, it's nothing serious, is it? I couldn't stand it if it were."

"Ella, if you stop interrupting I'll tell you."

"Sorry, you're quite right, carry on," I said, taking a deep breath in preparation for the news.

"Isobella Bridges, I'm very pleased to announce you are going to be an aunt."

Except for the one time when we were children and Jerry put a live frog down the back of my swimsuit, I can honestly say I have never squealed in a hysterical and embarrassing fashion. Until, that is, Jerry told me his news.

I could hear him on the other end of the line, laughing. "Good grief, let me move the telephone to the other ear. That one has gone quite deaf."

I laughed along with him. After the emotional trauma I had experienced recently this wholly unexpected but wonderful news was uplifting.

"Oh, Jerry, I am so very happy for you both and terribly excited to be an aunt. You must be absolutely thrilled.

"I'll say! Although I'm not sure it's really sunk in properly yet. I daresay I'll be a lot more nervous when the time comes."

"And when will that be?"

"Around Christmas time according to the doctor."

"Oh, Jerry, a Christmas baby. How perfect. Have you told anyone else yet?"

"I tried to get through to mother before I telephoned you but no dice. Have you heard from her at all?"

"Oh gosh, yes I have, listen to this..."

I quickly brought Jerry up to date with the news from France and told him I was going over there to assist. He was flabbergasted and I knew he would be torn between staying with his expectant wife and coming with me.

"Jerry, there's no need for you to come, you'll be better off staying at home where you're needed. And to be perfectly honest, darling, you'll not really be of much use as you'll no doubt spend most of your time worrying about leaving Ginny. Aunt Margaret and a friend of hers are accompanying me and I promise I'll keep you up to date with everything."

"Yes, you're right. I am loath to leave Ginny just now, but you must keep me informed. Day or night, just make sure you telephone or send a wire to let me know what's happening."

"Of course, and the news about the baby will cheer mother up no end. If you haven't managed to speak with her before I arrive, can I tell her the good news?"

"Naturally, but if I can't get through on the telephone I'll send a telegram to the hotel, so I expect she'll know by then."

"All right. Well, I must begin packing and I'm waiting for Aunt Margaret to call me back with details. Congratulations to you both again, it really is wonderful news. Tell

Ginny I will be along to see her as soon as I return. Goodbye, Jerry."

"Cheerio, old stick. Keep in touch."

I quickly left a message for Sergeant Baxter, my colleague at Scotland Yard, to inform him I would be away for the foreseeable future, and then went to wrestle with my luggage.

Halfway through my task I was interrupted by my part-time cook and housekeeper Mrs Parsons.

"'eavens, Miss Bridges, have we been burgled?" she said in horror, taking in the scenes of chaos around her.

"Not exactly, Mrs Parsons, although I'll forgive you for thinking so. I'm afraid I got a little carried away choosing what to pack."

"Well, you'll certainly not be needing this, Miss Bridges," she said, picking up a wool suit in shades of soft green. "It'll be a lot 'otter in France than here, you know. You'll keel over in the street of heatstroke if you wear this."

"Don't worry, Mrs Parsons, I wasn't planning on packing my winter wear. But I'm not sure how I will be travelling to France as yet. I'm waiting for my aunt to call back."

"Oh that's the reason I came up. Your aunt just rang..."

"I didn't hear the telephone."

"I was just passing the hall table when it went, only rang the once. Anyway I took down all the details," she said, rummaging in her apron pocket and handing me a sheet of paper. "I'll get on with your packing while you read the instructions."

I moved to the window seat while Mrs Parsons deftly sorted through my garments and returned the non-suitable items to my wardrobe. The further down my aunt's instructions I read the more my stomach started to tie itself in knots; a combination of nervous excitement and a little trepidation.

"Oh my word," I said breathlessly as I reached the end.

"I thought you'd be surprised," said Mrs Parsons, gently layering tissue paper between the folds of a satin evening dress. "Fancy hurtling yourself through the sky in nothing more than a fancy sardine tin! It's unnatural, that's what it is, not to mention dangerous. I mean how on earth does a thing that 'eavy stay up there, that's what I'd like to know? Rather you than me that's all I can say."

"Well, thank you for your insight, Mrs Parsons, most helpful," I said with a touch of sarcasm which my housekeeper missed completely.

"Don't mention it, Miss Bridges, it's my pleasure."

I smiled to myself. Mrs Parsons really was a dear old stick, missing a little on the tact front admittedly but she didn't have a malicious bone in her body. She was also doing me a huge favour. With the recent departure of my previous housekeeper, who it turned out wasn't a housekeeper at all, Mrs Parsons had stepped in to provide her services part-time and had also agreed to find me several new employees for the house, as well as help for her youngest son Tom who was my gardener. I would miss her when she left but no doubt I would see her around the village.

"Well, I suppose we had better get on. I'll need to set off quite early in the morning if I'm to get to Croydon Aerodrome in time for the noon flight. Now where on earth did I put my passport?..."

Chapter TWO

AS MY CHAUFFEUR TURNED onto Purley Way, I glanced out of the window and could make out in the distance the new Lido with its distinctive modern service building, blindingly white in the day's sunshine. Gently swaying palm trees, which I knew to be planted in man-made shingle beaches, added to the overall feel of a continental holiday, and as I watched I caught the sounds of laughter and merriment carried on the slight breeze through my open window. Set in four and a half acres of velvety lawned parkland, it had been opened in a furore of excitement the previous year and hailed a masterpiece of science and skill. As yet I had never managed to visit but having now seen it, I made a mental note to do so at the earliest opportunity, it looked like terrific fun.

Out of the other window and directly across the road from the Lido, I was mesmerised by the sight of several large metal aircraft awaiting their passengers, and was jolly relieved to note they looked nothing like sardine tins.

"Here we are then, Miss," my driver said, coming to a halt in front of the grand administration building. As I alighted, Aunt Margaret and Pierre approached; they had obviously been looking out for me.

"Ella, darling, perfect timing," Aunt Margaret said giving me hug as Pierre bestowed a lavish tip on my driver with which he was delighted, and organised a porter to deal with my luggage.

"Bonjour, Pierre," I said, leaning down and giving the small man a kiss on both cheeks. As per usual he was dressed in his trademark flamboyant style. This time he wore a lightweight cotton safari suit dyed to a glorious shade of turquoise with an equally vibrant raspberry shirt. Around his neck he'd tied a cravat in complimentary colours and perched on his head was a favourite fez with its gold tassel gently wafting in the breeze. By comparison I felt rather dowdy in my pale lemon sun-dress and matching jacket.

"Bonjour to you also, Ella, you look like a ray of sunshine today. Now what say we move inside? I believe it is time for cocktails, no?"

"Pierre, really," admonished my aunt. "It's barely time for elevenses. Besides I need to send a telegram to Elspeth to let her know of our arrival. I was unable to get through by telephone before we left."

Pierre shrugged. "Alas, I shall drink alone it seems."

"Poppycock," Aunt Margaret said in amusement when she saw I was wavering at Pierre's thoroughly dejected tone. "Don't let him fool you, Ella, he's already been waxing eloquent with a couple of his chums. He just wants the kudos of having a pretty girl on his arm."

"This is very true," he said nodding solemnly, while his eyes twinkled with merriment. "I have been rumbled. Well, adieu dear ladies, I will see you in a little while," and with a neat bow he sauntered in the direction of the lounge.

Aunt Margaret took my arm and, followed by the porter who was waiting patiently with my luggage trolley, we entered the booking hall. Officially opened only eight years previously, the hall was very stylish with a beautiful glass-domed roof which spilled light down into what would otherwise have been a dark interior, and an upper gallery where I saw patrons leaning on the geometric patterned railings.

Navigating our way passed the crowd at the newsagent's booth purchasing newspapers, magazines, postcards and cigarettes, we were surprised to hear a voice hailing my aunt.

"Margaret, is that you? Well, I never, it is. Fancy seeing you here of all places."

The owner of the voice was a very attractive, impeccably dressed woman with auburn hair and deep brown eyes, the twinkle in which immediately reminded me of my aunt.

"Emily, good heavens, how are you? It must be ten years

since I saw you last. Ella, this is Lady Ambrose. Emily, this is my niece, Isobella Bridges."

"Elspeth's girl? Gracious, I wouldn't have recognised you, dear. The last time I saw you, you had only just begun to walk."

She paused for a moment, then burst into gleeful laughter. "My, that was an idiotic thing to say, wasn't it? I should jolly well hope you'd changed since you were two."

"I'd certainly like to think so, Lady Ambrose," I said.

"Please call me Emily. Lady Ambrose makes me sound like my mother-in-law. So how is your mother? It's been a long time since I saw her."

"She's well, thank you. As a matter of fact that's why we are here. She lives in France now and I'm long overdue a visit. Are you headed there yourself?"

"I believe the French Riviera will be much too tame for Emily," my aunt said.

"Indeed," agreed Lady Ambrose. "I am an adventuress, Ella. It's Kenya and the African Savannah for me this time. Last year it was the pandas in China and before that, yaks in Tibet."

"Emily is a professional wildlife photographer, Ella, one of only three women in the world."

"And when I first started there was only me and it was an uphill struggle to be taken seriously. Eventually my work spoke for itself but I never forget how difficult it was. We women are just as good as men in many roles and thankfully things are changing for the better. Whatever it is you want to do, Isobella, then I highly recommend you going out and doing it."

At that moment we were approached by a young girl carrying a canvas bag and with a camera around her neck.

"Excuse me, Lady Ambrose, it's time to leave."

"Thank you, Cecily, I'll be just a moment."

"Ella already has a rather unique position, Emily," Aunt Margaret informed her as the young girl left.

"Oh do tell."

I told her.

She raised an eyebrow and said; "Now that is quite an achievement; well done, my dear. A chip off the old block eh, Margaret?" and winked at my aunt in a rather knowing way. My aunt smirked but said nothing. "Well toodle-pip, darlings, it's been lovely to catch up, albeit briefly. But I'll send an invitation when I return. I'd love you both to come and stay at Ferndale."

"What a fascinating woman," I said as we watched her retreating back.

"Isn't she just, and very kind and generous too. No doubt there will be an invitation through the door in the coming weeks. It will be lovely to see Ferndale again."

"Where is Ferndale?" I asked as we made our way to the telegraph office.

"Hereford. It's the Ambrose country seat, a great pile of Elizabethan splendour surrounded by acres of parkland designed by Capability Brown. You'll adore it, Ella. Ah, here we are. Now let's send a message your mother.

Having sent a telegram to Gardenia Villa, my mother's private home within the grounds of the White Hotel on Cap Ferrat, Aunt Margaret and I returned to the booking hall where we found Pierre perusing the newspapers.

"My beautiful travel companions return. Come along, ladies, I believe it is time to get weighed."

"Weighed?" I asked. "Whatever for?"

Pierre turned to me, "Ah, I forget this is your first time among the clouds, my dear Ella. We are to be weighed to ensure the aeroplane is not too heavy lest we find ourselves plummeting to earth like an Eagle diving for its prey."

"Pierre, really!" exclaimed Aunt Margaret. "Can't you see the girl is nervous enough? Ella, take no notice; it's a perfectly lovely experience, like having tea at the Ritz only up in the air."

Pierre patted my arm and looked suitably abashed. "I apologise, Ella. Your aunt is correct, there is nothing to concern yourself with; it is the height of luxury and a splendid way to travel."

I felt a small coil of alarm in my stomach. While Pierre had done his best to make light of his joke I still wasn't completely reassured. I was also surprised my aunt had noticed my fear. I thought I had done a rather good job of hiding my nervousness. I must practice my 'devil-may-care' attitude.

We moved back through the centre of the hall where I stopped to gaze at the time zone tower. It stood on a large octagonal base of polished wood, wide enough so that no amount of leaning forward could enable a person to reach the many clocks hanging on the central structure. It was fascinating to think that while it was late morning in London, on the opposite side of the world others were sleeping or perhaps just venturing out to dinner.

Far too soon I found myself at the scales where I was weighed and the numbers written in a small book by an officious looking clerk. We then proceeded to a long wooden counter where our passports were checked and our tickets issued together with a blue embarkation slip. I noticed a red label stuck to the front of my ticket and discovered it was my allocated seat. We were then escorted along a corridor to a door through which we found ourselves once more in the glorious sunshine.

Walking across the grass to the aircraft I was gripped by an odd feeling: the nearer it came the smaller it looked. Glancing at the number of my fellow passengers, not to mention the pilot and the staff as well as all our luggage, I was beginning to wonder how on earth we would all fit. Suddenly Mrs Parsons' sardine tin comment seemed uncannily apt.

I was handed up the three wooden steps into the aeroplane by a member of staff in his distinctive blue and white uniform with a Silver Wings pin affixed to his lapel, and glanced behind to see if Pierre needed my help, but he had managed, if somewhat awkwardly, to navigate their height. It struck me then how difficult life must be for our diminutive friend. I was duly escorted by a smartly attired steward to a table with a pristine white tablecloth.

"Welcome aboard, Miss," he said. "My name is Wilson, and I shall be your steward on the flight."

He asked if this was my first time on an aeroplane, and when I said it was, he pointed out a tray of boiled sweets. "I would recommend one of these, Miss, during ascent and descent. They help to equalise the pressure in the ear and the air pressure outside. Now, should you need anything at all just ring the service bell and I shall be pleased to assist."

I thanked him and shortly afterward my aunt and Pierre took their seats across from mine, both reaching for the sweets. I gazed around as the other passengers were getting settled and was gratified to note how similar it all was to a first class train carriage. From the crisp white curtains with their blue tie-backs, the plush comfortable seats upholstered in blue with white antimacassars, to the blue carpet running the length of the central gangway. There was even a selection of pictures on the walls depicting the various exotic destinations the airline flew to.

"How are you feeling, Ella?" my aunt asked.

"Actually I'm quite looking forward to the journey; it's much more civilised than I was expecting."

With a small jolt the aircraft began to make its way to the runway and Wilson arrived with the luncheon menus. So intent was I on perusing the offerings I barely registered we had come to a stop. Suddenly we were rushing forward at great speed, the momentum forcing me back into my seat, and seconds later we lifted into the air. I clutched at the table waiting for my stomach to catch up with the rest of me while the aeroplane tilted first, left then right, and eventually, much to my relief, leveled out. Wilson arrived with a carafe of water and took our orders and I took the opportunity to gaze at the vista below.

It was quite remarkable how quickly we had attained such a height and I felt a momentary giddiness at the reality of being so far above ground. I could see full grown trees no bigger than the shrubs in my garden and sheep the size of dandelion clocks. As we soared over the villages a great patchwork blanket of greens and yellows spread out, interspersed with rough tracks and hedges, and I spied several toy tractors working the fields. I thought at that moment, England had never looked more serene or beautiful.

Wilson arrived shortly after we began our journey over the channel and with nothing more interesting to see than a large body of water I turned my attention to the first course and in between mouthfuls asked my aunt how long the journey would take.

"The flight to Nice is approximately three hours, wouldn't you agree, Pierre?" Pierre nodded his assent. "Then it's a journey by road of no more than half an hour to the hotel."

"If we are lucky we may make it in time for afternoon tea," Pierre said.

I smiled. Only Pierre could think of afternoon tea while halfway through eating lunch. My aunt tutted, "This isn't a holiday, Pierre."

"Ah, my dear Maggie, of course I know this," Pierre said, patting her hand affectionately. "But there is very little we can do at the moment. We have answered the call of your sister as quickly as we could and we will, I am sure, solve this mystery of the missing colonel. I was only attempting to lighten things a little. There is no point worrying about that which at present we can do nothing about."

My aunt sighed and nodded. "Yes you're right of course. It's just the thoughts of poor Elspeth with the threat of a foreign prison hanging over her head. It's simply abominable."

"I'm sure it won't come to that, Aunt Margaret. It's ludicrous to think that on such a flimsy and tenuous link, a simple friendship between mother and the Colonel, the police would consider putting her in jail. I'm sure it's all just a silly misunderstanding. We'll sort it out once we get there."

"Thank you, dear," she said. But I noticed she barely touched the rest of the meal.

Sometime later, over coffee and some delicious French pastries, while Pierre was reading his newspaper and my aunt was taking a nap, I had the strangest sense of being watched. Looking toward the far end of the cabin I met the eye of a gentleman who, even though I had caught him out, continued to stare at me in the most uncomfortable way. I frowned and looked away but my curiosity was piqued and I looked back to find he was slowly walking in my direction, still boldly glaring at me.

As the strange man continued to advance, Wilson came to clear away the luncheon. With his arms laden he turned back towards the galley kitchen and I looked up to find the man passing my table, still staring. As he moved past me I glanced at my companions but they were blissfully unaware. Quickly I peered behind and found the man had completely disappeared, but Wilson had stopped in the gangway, his arms still carrying the remainder of our lunch, and was talking to a passenger at the next table. In the narrow space there was no way anyone could have passed the steward and there was no sign of him beyond. I checked the other tables but no one resembled the stranger; he had literally disappeared into thin air. My heart pounded at the thought I had seen an apparition. It was a gift and one I had come to accept, but with no knowledge of what the colonel looked like I automatically assumed the worst; that no matter how quickly we had rallied to my mother's aid we were already too late.

Chapter THREE

AUNT MARGARET AWOKE and Pierre shuffled and folded his newspaper just as the announcement that we were coming in to land came crackling over the Tannoy system.

I didn't mention the stranger as it would do no good to worry them, and the explanation would have taken far too long as neither were fully aware of my proclivity for seeing ghosts. As the aeroplane began to drop and the wings once more began to tilt I made the mistake of looking out of the window. The view I am sure was breathtaking but the speed with which the ground was coming up to meet us was too much. So I sat back and closed my eyes, furiously sucking a boiled sweet and waiting for the bump, which Aunt Margaret had forewarned me about, that would let me know we were safely back on land.

It seemed to take an age and my knuckles were white with clinging to the arms of my chair for so long, but eventually we landed with a heavy bump, skipped into the air once, twice, then finally landed permanently. I let out the breath I had inadvertently been holding and opened my eyes.

"Landing isn't quite the same as taking off, is it?" Aunt Margaret said with a smile.

Disembarking, I glanced round for the staring man on the off chance I was mistaken about his ghostly form but there was no sign of him.

"Have you lost something, Ella?"

I shook my head, "No nothing like that, Aunt Margaret." She looked at me sharply but said nothing more.

As we moved through the arrivals hall I was astounded by the reception Pierre received. It was apparent that the small, private man I knew was a big cheese on this side of the channel. Everyone from the lowliest porter to the manager knew who he was and insisted on greeting him and shaking his hand. A number of them even asked for his autograph.

"Pierre is very famous here," my aunt explained unnecessarily.

"I had no idea. It's a tad worrying considering our reason for coming."

"There's no need to concern yourself on that score,

Ella. Pierre will be the soul of discretion, but he has a way of unlocking doors which would otherwise be firmly closed to the likes of us. I expect we'll be very glad of the association and his knowledge should things become difficult."

"Do you think it will be difficult? I may have a few solved cases under my belt but I'm quite at sea here. I know nothing of French Law or the logistics of evidence gathering and have no jurisdiction or support at all. I don't even speak the language. I'm beginning to wish I'd asked Sergeant Baxter along."

"Well, as you and Pierre firmly told me on the aeroplane there is no use worrying about it until we get there. Once we've spoken with your mother we'll know more about what we are dealing with and can plan a way forward. And I daresay Baxter would feel much the same as you do should he have come along."

I nodded in agreement, Sergeant Baxter as my colleague at Scotland Yard, was astute and experienced and a wonderful source of support and knowledge back in England, but I daresay he would feel as alien as I did, here in France. However I took solace in the fact I could always telephone him for advice if I needed to.

We trailed after Pierre as he magically worked the crowd with Gallic affability like a consummate politician, asking after husbands, wives, grandchildren and even pets. He remembered the names of the airport staff, enquired about their health and was genial and gracious and full of bonhomie with everyone. Eventually we were ushered into a private room where our passports and paperwork were quickly stamped, then led through to a separate area outside where a limousine and driver were waiting, our luggage apparently having been rushed through especially quickly due to Pierre's celebrity.

"Goodness!" I exclaimed, admiring the luxury vehicle.

"Pierre goes everywhere in style here," my aunt said as we settled into our seats. "Unless of course he's incognito, then he could be on a bicycle or pushing a wheelbarrow and you wouldn't know it was him."

Pierre hearing the end of the comment said, "I have never pushed a wheelbarrow in my life before. I have however ridden in one."

"Ah yes, my mistake; it was the gypsy handcart you were pushing."

"And in which you were riding," Pierre replied with his customary twinkle.

I laughed at their banter but refrained from asking questions. I wouldn't get any answers. One day perhaps I would learn what had brought these two unlikely friends together and learn more about their escapades, but for now I was quite content to sit back and observe. As we pulled away and started out along the coast road I glimpsed a man standing in the shade of a tree opposite, staring at the car. My stomach twisted and the hairs on the back of my neck stood up;

it was the stranger from the aeroplane and at his feet was a black cat, my black cat in actual fact. It could only mean one thing; there had been a suspicious death. I only hoped it wasn't the colonel.

The journey to the hotel took exactly thirty minutes as my aunt had said. I'd barely registered the beautiful scenery as we journeyed — just snippets of an azure sea with diamond-like flashes where the sun glinted off the water and the riot of colour from the bougainvillea and azaleas. My mind was on other things. As the driver parked at the entrance, Pierre said, "Now I have booked a suite at the hotel for the duration. Gaston will leave me here and take you both on to the villa. I will meet you there in the morning for breakfast. Adieu, my friends."

Having watched Pierre received into the open arms of the manager and several staff who were delighted to have such a celebratory figure grace their hotel, Gaston proceeded to take my aunt and me to Gardenia Villa.

"Do you remember coming here when you were a child?" my aunt asked as we meandered our way through the lush gardens and parkland that made up the hotel's many acres. "Not this hotel, of course. It had barely begun to be constructed then, but this area?"

I shook my head. "Mother has told me she and Father brought Jerry and me here for a holiday when we were young but I remember nothing of it at all."

"She has very fond memories of those times, you know. I do believe it was the reason she chose to move here."

"It is very beautiful," I said as we passed glimpses of secret gardens through the greenery.

"Yes. I do so hope we get a happy ending to this mystery. I would so hate for the memories to be overshadowed by anything sinister. It would completely ruin the place for Elspeth."

This last was said in quiet tones as though she was speaking to herself and I knew she wasn't expecting an answer, but it gave me a sense of urgency coupled with mild panic. I fervently hoped I was up to the task for I was almost certain something sinister had already occurred.

As we pulled up outside the villa mother came tripping lightly down the steps.

"Ella, darling, I'm so happy you're here. You've no idea how glad I am." She gave me a tight hug before pulling away and turning to her sister. "Margaret, thank you for coming; it's such a relief your being here."

"How are you bearing up, Elspeth?"

Mother sighed deeply and rubbed her forehead. "Well I'm worried, Margaret, and that insufferable policeman is making everything worse. But let's not talk out here. I'll have your luggage sent to your rooms and once you've freshened up we can have tea on the patio."

As the butler and a maid saw to our luggage, I turned to thank Gaston and my aunt brought out her purse but Gaston shook his head.

"No need, Madame, Monsieur DuPont has seen to everything." He tipped his hat and returned to the vehicle.

As we turned to go inside I surveyed the villa. It was a two story building in brilliant white with shutters on the windows painted in turquoise, which were complimented beautifully by a mature wisteria in full bloom. A riot of magenta and soft pink bookended the residence in the form of large bougainvillea bushes, and a hedge of lilac with its silver foliage was planted at either side of the steps. The whole was encapsulated with tall pine, cypress and palm, with low lying box nestled at intervals, which eventually gave onto the forest that made up a large proportion of the peninsula. I adored it.

Inside my first impressions were of a cool light interior, gilded mirrors and sparkling chandeliers, but I took in little more than that as the maid escorted me up the wide wooden staircase with a wrought iron balustrade to my room. Again the feeling of a light and airy space with all the comforts of home were apparent but my uppermost thought was my mother and the disappearance of the colonel, so I was quick to freshen up and change. My aunt must have been of the same mind as she was exiting the room adjacent to mine at the same time and we made our way out to the garden together. Mother was already waiting under a shady pergola.

"There you both are. Come and sit down and tell me what news you have from home. We can discuss other matters shortly. I'd just like to have a little time where I can pretend everything is normal."

"Actually I do have some very exciting news," I said. "You're going to be a grandmother."

She stared at me, a smile frozen on her lips while the teacup my aunt was holding halted halfway toward her mouth.

I burst out laughing. "Well, really! I don't mean me. Ginny is expecting and due around Christmas time."

"Thank heavens for that," exclaimed my aunt. "I thought I was going to have to cart you off to a convent in the Outer Hebrides or some such place."

We all laughed. "You wouldn't." I said.

She shook her head. "No of course not... I'd just leave you here."

That comment caused even more mirth.

"Oh you have no idea how wonderful it is to be laughing again," my mother said, wiping her eyes. "And what glorious news. I am so happy for them both and to think I will be a grandmother at last. I'll try and telephone later but the lines have been down and I don't know if they have been fixed as yet."

"Jerry did say he'd been trying to get hold of you but

to no avail; he really did want to tell you himself. He said he'd send a telegram to the hotel. Have you not received one?"

"No I haven't, such a shame. I would have loved to have spoken with them both. But at least I know now and I expect the lines will be working again soon. I will make arrangements to come and stay nearer the time. We can spend Christmas all together. It's been a long while since we've done that, and we'll have much to celebrate with a new member of the family. I just hope..." She stopped and I knew what she was thinking. I took her hand.

"We'll find him, mother."

"I do hope so, Ella; it's been torment not knowing. I'm convinced something dreadful has happened but the authorities just dismiss my concerns as those of a neurotic woman. I rather think they are of the opinion Edward disappeared to get away from me. It's not true of course but Perret is that sort of man."

"Do you feel up to telling us what happened, Elspeth?"

"Of course, let us finish our tea and you can catch me up with everything, Ella, then we'll move indoors and I'll explain everything from the start.

While my aunt and mother were settling themselves in the expansive drawing room I went back to retrieve a notebook and pen, and finally had time to take in the opulent but welcoming bedroom. The walls were paneled floor to ceiling and painted in a soft cream which matched the wall to wall carpet. To the left was a marble fire place with a beautiful old mirror set into an overmantel reaching from the mantelpiece to the ceiling. In one corner sat a comfortable armchair upholstered in duck egg blue with a fringed base, behind which a Tiffany lamp was artfully placed on a tall stand, and in the wall next to it cream-painted inset shelving, with two cupboards at the base, displayed various knick-knacks and several framed photographs of the family. Two large windows dominated one wall with light curtains and a valance of the softest pink, but it was the bed on a raised dais that was the centrepiece. Set against the wall in between the windows it was a four poster curtained without fuss in the same blue as the chair, with an ornate filigree style bed-head in burnished gold. It all spoke to my mother's good taste and style and I wasn't surprised at how immediately I felt at home.

I'd already discovered my personal bathroom and dressing room, but there was a further door I'd yet to explore. Peering through, I saw it was a small private sitting room tastefully decorated in similar tones to the bedroom. It was beautiful but with so much to do, and new surroundings to explore, not to mention glorious sunny weather I doubted it would get used.

I returned to the downstairs drawing room to find Aunt Margaret and my mother reminiscing over framed photographs displayed on the white grand piano.

"And here we all are at the beach when the children were small. It's not far from here. I'll take you if we get the chance," mother was saying. "Ah, Ella, do you remember this?" She handed me the frame and I peered at the black and white grainy picture of Jerry and myself sitting on a blanket with my mother and father.

"No, I don't remember but we were obviously having a good time if the huge smiles are anything to go by. Who took the photograph?"

"Oh! Do you know I have no idea, isn't that strange? Of course it was a long time ago. Such a lovely time we had."

I smiled and she returned the frame to the piano. As we settled onto the settee and chairs, arranged to give a perfect view of the garden through the open patio doors beneath the three large stone arches, we agreed that rather than go out to dinner we would prefer to have a casual supper here at the villa.

"That would suit me better. I think I will feel quite washed out once I've told you everything. Now where would you like me to start?"

"Perhaps from the time the colonel arrived. Can you remember when it was?"

"Yes, late February. A friend, Lily Cranbrook — they

have a villa further along the bluff — had telephoned to see if I wanted to have dinner up at the hotel; her husband was away and she was rather at a loose end."

"And he was there?"

"Yes. He took the table next to ours and Lily introduced us both and we began to talk. It's a friendly expatriate community here; some have residential suites at the hotel itself, others have villas as I do within the grounds, but there are also those who have private homes elsewhere who frequent the restaurant. Most of us know one another well or are at least on nodding terms so a new face is always interesting."

I nodded, making notes. "When did you see him next?"

"Let me see... it was several days later. I had taken a trip to the village and was just having coffee at a little cafe when he approached and asked if he could join me. As clichéd as it sounds, it was the beginning of a wonderful friendship, and we've spent time together or spoken every day since."

"Has he ever gone off for a few days like this before?"

"Yes, he's a keen amateur photographer and several times has arranged a spur of the moment overnight stay if his wanderings have kept him late, or if he's found something he wants to continue with the following day. But he has always telephoned to let me know."

"And you never accompanied him on his photography trips?"

"Not the ones further afield. He said he would be poor

company and that I should most likely be bored and he would feel terribly guilty about not giving me his full attention. He has rather a one track mind on these occasions and spends a long time walking about looking for the perfect shot. I must admit he was probably right, but he always carried one of his cameras with him wherever we went."

"He has more than one?"

"Oh yes, he has several, one a rather remarkable little thing which hardly looks like a camera at all. Of course once you realise what it is, it's quite obvious. Very clever, but I've only seen him use it once."

"And when was that?"

"We'd gone to Nice for the day and were just casually walking, looking in shop windows and that sort of thing when he stopped and took a picture. I asked what had interested him as I couldn't see anything remotely photogenic; just the shopping street, a few cars and pedestrians, but of course I don't have a photographer's eye. He said he rather liked the look of the old building across the street. I couldn't see the attraction myself; it was nothing particularly interesting."

I caught my Aunt's eye and she raised an eyebrow but remained silent.

"Does he have any family?"

My mother shook her head. "No. He was an only child and his parents are both deceased. He never married although I believe there was an engagement at one point which was broken. I didn't ask the reasons. It may have been the war."

"Perhaps we could move forward to the day he disappeared. Where were you and when did you realise he had gone?"

She glanced at her watch. "It's nearly seven o'clock. I'll just see about supper first, then we can carry on."

She left the room in search of the maid and I turned to my aunt.

"What are your thoughts, Aunt Margaret?"

"Much the same as yours, I expect. There's more to the colonel than meets the eye but I don't think Elspeth is aware of it. However, it could be something totally innocent. We'll have to do some digging, I'm afraid."

I agreed with her. There was no doubt in my mind that my mother and the colonel were good friends and that he admired and respected her a great deal. But there seemed to be something that didn't quite ring true. I sighed and made a few more notes just as mother returned.

"I've arranged for a cold supper in half an hour. Will that be enough time, do you think?"

"Yes I think so."

"Well, the day he disappeared we had gone to our weekly art class. With his keen eye for photography I thought he would be rather good at it. I've been attending for a long while now and thoroughly enjoy it, but as you can see it wasn't quite his forte." She indicated an unframed canvas leaning against a wall which I had missed. It was a scene of the harbour with a few boats and a jetty done in oils. While colourful it was rather primitive and quite amateurish.

"He gave it to me as a gift. I'm not sure what to do with it. It was his first attempt at painting with oils. He much preferred watercolour as a medium, but even then he admitted he wasn't particularly talented."

"Better not let Pierre see it," my aunt laughed.

"Of course your artist friend! That's probably very wise; I'll keep it well hidden."

"So he went missing from your art class?" I asked.

"Not from the class itself. We'd been there all morning and had been chatting to our fellow students and everything seemed perfectly normal. We walked back part of the way together, then he went on to the hotel while I came home. We had made arrangements for dinner that evening but he never showed up and that was the last I saw of him. He would never have left me sitting in the restaurant alone, Ella, that's why I'm sure something dreadful has happened."

"Did you ask the manager where he was?"

"Of course, but this is the most worrying thing. He said Edward had gone out that morning but no one had seen him return and his rooms hadn't been disturbed from when the maid had gone in that morning. He told me not to worry; perhaps he had missed his train or something."

"When did you inform the police he was missing?"

"I telephoned from the hotel that night but was treated as a foolish woman. They said he needed to have been missing for much longer before they would consider it seriously. I tried, Ella, I really did but they just wouldn't listen. I spent a sleepless night, then went to the police station the next morning and demanded something be done. Eventually Perret ushered me into his office and... Well to cut a long story short he dismissed my worries, although he was overly polite about it, if you understand what I mean?" I nodded.

"I've telephoned every day since except today to ask what is being done. The last time I had the telephone put down on me. Can you imagine? I was furious. They seem to think he's away somewhere having a nice time and taking his photographs, but had forgotten to let me know. And do you know what they said when I informed them he had failed to arrive for our dinner date? That I had most likely misunderstood him and had got the day mixed up."

"I'm quite appalled at the response you've received. If our English police behaved like this then they would soon be out of a job. They are either being extremely lazy, deliberately obtuse with you and the colonel both being foreigners, or they are hiding something. But whatever the reason, I shall pay this detective Perret a visit tomorrow and rest assured he will not be able to arrest you, mother. He's just throwing his weight around."

"What I don't understand," said Aunt Margaret "is what he was going to arrest you *for*, Elspeth?"

"Well, as far as I understand it, it's because I was so close to Edward and was the last to see him. He said if Edward's disappearance proved to be serious, then a case could be made to say I had something to do with it. He intimated that I would not like a French prison at all. In fact he went into quite graphic detail as to what I could expect."

"But that's appalling."

"Yes, I did feel quite threatened."

"I'm not surprised mother, I would too. But rest assured he has no grounds to arrest you. I rather feel it was a hollow threat in order to stop you from demanding they do their job. Now there's one other question I need to ask then we can enjoy our supper."

I took a deep breath. It was the question I most dreaded the answer to and the reason I had left it until last.

"What does Colonel Summerfield look like?"

"It's odd I don't have a photograph of him, isn't it, considering his hobby. He's forty nine," I stopped her with a raised hand.

"And he's retired you say?"

"Yes. It is quite young I suppose, but I believe there's some family money. Of course it's not the sort of thing one discusses so I know nothing more. He's tall, distinguished looking and carries himself well. Dark hair with threads of silver at his temples and thinning slightly at his crown. He's quite dark skinned too, more so since he's been here with all the sunshine and fresh air, brown eyes and cleanly shaven. It doesn't sound much when you distill it down like that, does it? But he is a handsome man and quite debonair."

My heart thudded as I dutifully made my notes, and kept my head down while I did so to avoid the possibility of my mother seeing the fear in my eyes, for she had just described perfectly the staring man on the aeroplane.

Chapter FOUR

PIERRE ARRIVED FOR BREAKFAST at exactly eight thirty the following morning and was shown into the breakfast room by the maid. "Monsieur DuPont, Madame," she said with a curtsy.

My mother rose to greet him, her hand outstretched, "Monsieur DuPont, what an absolute pleasure to meet you at last. My sister has told me so much about you."

Pierre took her hand and kissed it, "The pleasure is all mine, Mrs Bridges. Let us not stand on ceremony; you must call me Pierre."

"And I am Elspeth. Please come and join us."

As we helped ourselves to the impressive continental breakfast, the three of us brought Pierre up to date with our previous night's conversation. He listened intently, nodding at intervals, but made no remarks. He then told us what he had learned.

"Much of what you have told me I have also confirmed. Colonel Summerfield has not been here long; he is a keen amateur photographer, discreet and personable and is well liked by staff and patrons both. The manager is most upset at his disappearance, more so since he knows I am concerned."

"You've raised us all in importance, I take it?" my aunt said sardonically.

Pierre gave a little shrug. "It cannot be helped, naturally your association with me will do that. But I have asked the manager to be circumspect, which he has assured me he will and I have no reason to doubt him. It will after all do us no favours with the police if you were to become too important. Our investigation needs to be kept low-key so as not to frighten our adversary."

"So you do think something has happened to Edward?" my mother asked with a sigh of relief.

"I do, Madame. It is most suspicious for him to disappear and leave you stranded at the dinner table. Not the way a gentleman behaves and according to the hotel manager, Colonel Summerfield is a gentleman."

"Oh he is," my mother agreed. "Very much so."

"Now we need to make a plan of action, Madame. Ella, what are your thoughts?"

"I certainly wish to see this detective Perret. He is either exceptionally shrewd or a complete fool, but I shan't know until I meet him. I do wonder if I should tell him my connection to Scotland Yard though. Do you think it would be wise or foolish, Pierre?"

"Yes, it is a difficult choice. We don't want to display our hand too soon, but also we need the help of the policemen to look for the colonel. I think you will need to use your discretion, my young friend, but perhaps downplay your association, yes? It will do no good to threaten him; most likely it will have an adverse effect. Frenchmen are proud and Perret will not like being told what to do by a woman, particularly a foreign woman."

I nodded. "Yes I can do that. I'll go this afternoon. But first I think we should pay a visit to the art school."

"You think there's something there, Ella?" Aunt Margaret asked.

"I doubt it but he disappeared shortly after leaving so I want to make sure."

"Ah yes, the art school, very interesting. They hold exhibitions at the gallery in the town if I'm not mistaken?" said Pierre.

"Yes they do," my mother confirmed. "Not our amateurish work of course, but some of the better ones have been on display. It's to generate interest in the classes more than anything else; they aren't for sale."

"So shall we all go along?" I asked to the table at large. Aunt Margaret and my mother said yes, but Pierre declined, citing an appointment.

As we were finishing our breakfast the maid entered. "Excuse me, Madame, but what would you like me to do with this painting?"

Pierre turned around. "Mon Dieu!" he exclaimed with extreme distaste, and I heard my aunt mutter, "So much for that idea."

"Pierre, it was done by Colonel Summerfield at the art school and given to mother as a gift," I said hurriedly to avoid the forthcoming insults, but my mother shook her head.

"Ella, don't worry, Edward is fully aware it's quite dreadful."

"It is," Pierre said, nodding quite solemnly which caused us all to laugh.

"Do you have any of your paintings here?" I asked my mother.

"Good heavens no, I'm sure mine are little better than Edward's effort. They're still at the school. I'll show them to you as they were intended as gifts."

Pierre was still intent on looking at the picture. "It is quite odd."

"Yes, I think we're all agreement about that, Pierre," Aunt Margaret said.

He gave her a withering look, "It is an odd size, not what I would expect. Most unusual and somehow... familiar, but alas it eludes me and is likely unimportant. I wish you all adieu, my friends. Thank you for a delightful breakfast, Elspeth. I shall see you all this evening. I may have news."

By the time we had said goodbye to Pierre and were ready to leave it was still three quarters of an hour before the art school was due to open, so mother suggested we take in the sights and walk. The art school, while not within the grounds of the hotel, was just on the outskirts and could be approached using the coastal footpath.

"It's a very pretty walk and gives you wonderful views of the peninsula and beaches," she said.

We went out through the French doors across the patio and followed the pathway down through the garden, under a tunnel of sweet smelling greenery, to some winding steps which led to one of two gates.

"The gate further along leads down a set of private steps cut into the hillside to the beach. There's another gate at the bottom but they take the same key."

"You have your own private beach?" I asked.

"No, the beach is for everyone's use, but I have private access from the villa. All the villas at this side do."

"So no one but villa owners can use the coastal path?" I found this difficult to comprehend but I couldn't work out the geography.

"Not at all, there is a public footpath a little lower down. It's only the section past this side of the private residences which is for the residents only. There are some quite well known people who have villas here, and a lot of wealth; it prevents trespassing."

As we walked, mother explained the geography. The hotel was on the crown of the peninsula and her villa was to the left looking from the mainland. The footpath circumnavigated the entire peninsula, but the section we traversed continued left and would eventually take us out of the hotel grounds via a manned gate. From there it was but a five minute walk to the art school.

The gentle stroll was indeed a very pretty one and incredibly tranquil. We were awarded tantalising glimpses of grand villas and gardens to our left, and to the right the craggy Provençal coastline with its cobalt blue waters. The gentle susurration of the waves on the shore murmured continuously in the background and was overlaid with laughter rising from the sandy coves and the occasional cry of a gull on the wing. We walked under tropical palms and sweet-smelling umbrella pines, and were entranced by the bobbing of the small fishing boats on the water and the impressive silhouette of the lighthouse built by Napoleon III.

"Here we are," my mother said as we reached a large gate with a small booth to one side where a security guard was sitting. He spoke briefly to my mother in French, tipped his hat at Aunt Margaret and me, and then opened the gate for us to pass.

"I didn't realise you spoke the language so fluently, mother?"

"Neither did detective Perret. How else do you think I knew he thought me a neurotic Englishwoman? Besides it's the correct thing to do. It's also quite impossible to live in a country where you cannot understand half of what is said."

"You didn't let on to Perret you understood him?"

"No, of course not, why would I?"

"Well, that could prove to be jolly useful, don't you think, Ella?" asked my aunt.

"Indeed. But your staff were all speaking English?"

"Only when I have English guests, Ella. It would be the height of rudeness otherwise, don't you agree?"

I did, but it would have been nice to be able to converse with them in their own language, even if it was something quite innocuous, and I was determined by the time I left to have at least picked up some basic phrases.

❋

The art school was housed in a magnificent old villa, bequeathed by the former owner who was a keen patron of the arts, and was currently run by a very attractive, chic and flamboyant Frenchwoman called Clementine Dubois. She greeted my mother like a long lost friend, grasping her shoulders and planting a delicate kiss on both cheeks, then proceeded to chatter at such a speed I believe even my mother was hard pressed to understand every word. But the meaning was clear; she was overjoyed to see my mother.

Switching to English she asked, "Elspeth, is there news? Is that why you have come?" Her eyes took on a deepening worried look which I saw mirrored in my mother's.

"No, Clementine, there is no news yet," she said sadly and squeezed her friend's hand. "I've brought my daughter Ella and my sister Margaret."

"Ah, of course!" she said, turning to us with a smile.

My aunt and I stuck out our hands both being a little more reserved and less tactile than my mother, but Clementine Dubois just laughed.

"Oh you English! But we are in France now, no?"

She proceeded to give us both similarly enthusiastic greetings, kissing the air in the general direction of our cheeks. "Now, are you here for the lesson?"

"Not today. Perhaps another day, but I would like to show them round?"

"Mais oui, of course. Sadly I have a class but you know where everything is, please make yourselves at home. Au revoir, my friends. Elspeth, ma chére, if you have news do let me know?"

My mother nodded and after another brief hug Clementine left to attend her students.

As we walked through the beautifully landscaped gardens, mother explained the school was one of the most prestigious in France, catering to an elite section of the most talented individuals. There were various youngsters milling about or talking in hushed groups, several sitting on the central lawns, sketch pads in hand, or propped up against the fountain, reading. We passed a number concentrating on canvases propped on large easels and their talent took my breath away.

As we moved further through the gardens away from the main building I spied another smaller structure tucked into an expanse of greenery; it was here the lessons for the amateur enthusiasts were conducted. We approached a covered portico where several mature students were working on large canvasses propped on easels, and through the patio doors leading to an indoor studio several more could be seen hard at work. Meandering through them all and stopping occasionally to give advice in a low whisper, was a middle aged man in loose cotton trousers and a dark blue smock, with a beret perched on wild grey hair. Pince-nez precariously balanced on the end of his nose and fastened by a long gold chain leading to a gold pin affixed to his breast completed the look. I was in no doubt this was the teacher.

"Oh dear," my mother murmured beside me.

"What is it?" I whispered.

"It's Monsieur Valin; he is today's teacher. I was rather hoping it would be someone else. He is a little difficult, speaks no English and under no circumstances are you to address him as anything but Maestro."

"Good lord," Aunt Margaret said in hushed tones. "A large ego by the sounds of it."

Mother nodded. "Yes. He is very knowledgeable and not a bad teacher, although somewhat impatient. I rather get the impression he feels this is all beneath him."

"Will he let you show us around, Elspeth?"

"We can but try. It will all depend on his mood; let us hope he is in an agreeable state of mind."

Monsieur Valin, rather rudely I thought, didn't reply to my mother's polite greeting but shrugged and waved a hand somewhat brusquely in the direction of the studio when she had finished speaking. She beckoned us forward and I glanced at Monsieur Valin, but he'd already moved away to attend another pupil.

The studio space inside was huge, with a scruffy wooden floor splattered with a rainbow of colours and well lit with windows on three sides and a partial glass roof. Cupboards and shelving dominated the back wall and were full of every sort of paint, pencil and paper imaginable. A stack of unused small canvasses were propped against the shelves and a free standing wooden unit housed jars full of brushes. There were only five people painting here and mother introduced us to them all. We nodded politely and admired their work. One in particular, a pretty rendition in oils of the outer courtyard fountain, caught my aunt's eye.

"Hello, Elsie," my mother said and introduced us.

Elsie was a small bird-like woman with a shock of unruly snowy white curls, tamed somewhat by a felt hat bedecked with ribbons and flowers. She had a sweet little face and shrewd eyes with a twinkle not unlike Pierre's. She was dressed in the fashion of thirty years ago in soft grey accented with lace, but it suited her admirably.

"I must say you have a natural talent and a very good eye. The attention to detail is splendid," said my aunt and I agreed with her.

"Oh you are too kind," Elsie replied. "I used to dabble a bit as a young girl but nothing too serious; one didn't in those days you know. This is for my niece. I only hope it arrives this time. The last one got lost, I'm afraid."

"Oh not the still life with peonies, Elsie? What a shame! It was beautiful, and such a lot of work," my mother sympathised. "I do hope it turns up eventually."

"I wouldn't rely on it," a cultivated English baritone said behind us. "The post is simply abominable. I had two of mine go missing last year. I was jolly pleased with them too."

"Oh dear, Mr Feltham, how awful for you. I must admit I have had letters go missing on occasion, most annoying. But I suppose we are obliged to put up with it if we live here," mother said. After a short conversation where the state of the French Post Office was duly lambasted, we moved on. I was quite glad as Monsieur Valin had just entered and he looked quite cross.

"Are all the amateur students' expatriates, Elspeth?"

"Yes, I think that's why Valin despises it so," she said out of earshot of the Maestro himself who was leaning over Mr Feltham's shoulder and jabbing with his finger.

"Where are your paintings, mother?"

"They are stored in this room over here."

We moved in that direction and just as she was about to grasp the handle, we heard an angry voice gabbling in French behind us. It was Monsieur Valin, in a terrible temper. My mother answered in French but he flung his arms in the air then pointed in the direction of the exit. It was apparent he wanted us to leave, but at that moment Clementine arrived.

She laid a placating hand on Valin's arm and spoke in gentle French but he was not to be appeased. Heated words were exchanged and he stormed out of the door in a fit of pique.

Clementine turned to us, an apologetic look on her face and a tired smile. "Please forgive my colleague. It is the artistic temperament."

"I am sorry, Clementine, I realise we must be in the way

and understand it's difficult for him to teach while we are wandering around. We should go."

"Non! I will not hear of it. You are most welcome here. Yes, you are right, this is what he says, how do I expect him to teach under these circumstances? But it is an excuse and he needs to remember the students here are private and paying to be taught well. Without you all we could not sponsor those with raw talent who do not have the means. It is an important and vital part of the school. Do not worry. He will calm down and all will be forgotten. Now let us show your talent to your family." She unlocked the door and we entered a sort of combined storeroom and gallery.

Behind the door on the same wall, there were floor to ceiling shelves with uprights like a concertina, and in each individual space there was a plain canvas ready for use. Every size imaginable was available with the largest at the bottom and the smallest at the top. The shelving was split in half top to bottom but to my uneducated eye there was no discernible difference between them. I asked Clementine about them.

"This is Valin's responsibility. This half I believe contain those which the school has bought and this half is the donations. There is a company in Nice who let us have slight imperfections for nothing, it is very good of them. They are like this so we can keep a note of the stock for the bookkeeping." She shrugged and smiled. "Very mundane I think, but the art school, while a centre for creative excellence, is also a business."

"Here we are," my mother called from the other side of the room.

She had taken two small paintings in oil and stood them up on a small table side by side. One was a scene of the town square in summer sunshine, with a row of ancient shops, trees and people walking along the pavement or sitting outside at cafes. The other a view of the walk along the coastal path with the cobalt sea and the glinting sun on the water, and bright-coloured fishing boats so realistically rendered I could almost see them bobbing over the waves.

"Well you have been hiding your talent, Elspeth," my aunt remarked.

"Mother, these are beautiful, and I agree with Aunt Margaret. I didn't realise you were so skilled."

"Oh there are better students than I, but I am pleased with how these two worked out; earlier efforts were quite poor, and I had you two in mind when I did them. I was going to arrange to have them posted on but considering the previous conversation perhaps you would like to take them back with you on the aeroplane?"

There was no doubt about which she had done for us, as my aunt reached out for the street scene and I the seascape.

"Oh, mother, I'd love it."

"As would I, Elspeth. I think Pierre would be suitably impressed with them too and that's saying something."

"Clementine, would you be so kind as to arrange delivery to the villa? We are going on to have lunch now and can't possibly carry them with us."

"Of course, ma chére, I shall have them wrapped and delivered to you soon."

Leaving the school we passed an open window and heard Valin in a heated conversation on the telephone.

"What is he saying, Elspeth?" Aunt Margaret asked as we walked slowly below the window out of sight.

"He is complaining that we have been interrupting his lesson and wandering around in the storeroom. He's furious that Clementine allowed it and is threatening to leave," she whispered. "He has given an ultimatum: Clementine or himself."

"Well, let us hope whoever he is speaking to calls his bluff and takes him up on his offer."

However that wasn't the outcome and what happened next shocked us all to the core.

Chapter FIVE

※

WE HAD LUNCH OUTSIDE a quaint old cafe under a brightly striped canopy and mother explained how to get to the Sûreté. It was time to meet detective Perret.

"Be careful, Ella, the man is difficult and I think quite dangerous; should he sense a weakness he will pounce."

And with those words still ringing in my ear, I set off.

The building which housed the local police was an old one, rendered and painted in a soft pink with white doors. I entered to the tinkle of a bell and approached a dark wooden counter behind which was a uniformed officer. He looked me up and down in a supercilious manner, no doubt taking in my dress and immediately surmising I was a foreigner.

"Oui?"

"Good afternoon. Do you speak English?"

"A little."

"I'm looking for detective Perret. Is he available?"

He arched a brow. "*Lieutenant* Perret is not here."

I sighed inwardly; already I had made a mistake.

"I apologise. Do you know when the lieutenant will return?"

"Non."

I gritted my teeth at his insouciance and smiled politely. I had no doubt he understood me perfectly well but was being deliberately obtuse.

"Well, in that case I would like to speak to someone in charge. It's about a missing person, a case with which I believe Lieutenant Perret is familiar."

"He is not here."

"I know, you have already told me. But who is here that I can speak to?"

"Perhaps I can help, Mademoiselle?" said an accented voice in English behind me.

"Capitaine," the man at the desk said, a plum hue rising to his face.

I turned. "Good afternoon. You are in charge here?"

"Yes. I am Captain Robillard, Mademoiselle. You have a missing friend? We can talk in my office, come. Belett, please bring tea."

"Oui, Capitaine," said an unctuous voice from behind the counter and I thought how aptly named he was. While my knowledge of French was limited, I did know the word for weasel, thanks to a French school friend when I was a child, and a well-known nursery rhyme.

Seated in the sparsely appointed office I told the captain about the missing colonel. He took notes while I talked but asked few questions.

"And you say Perret knows about this?"

"Yes. He spoke to my mother although I'm afraid he wasn't very helpful."

The captain frowned. "One moment please."

He went to the door and called in French to Belett. Returning to his seat he said, "I have asked for Perret's file on the case. At the least there should be a missing person form."

A moment later the door opened and Belett arrived with a tea tray. Placing it on the end of the desk next to the telephone with the utmost care, he then passed a slim manila file to his superior.

"Merci, Belett. That will be all."

He poured, handed me a cup, then went back to the file. I sipped my tea while he was familiarising himself with what the report contained. It seemed an interminable length of time before he lowered it and looked at me.

"It is not satisfactory and maybe not what you expect to hear but Perret has made some inquiries. According to witnesses, your Colonel Summerfield was seen leaving the hotel and walking to the village. Another witness says he got into a taxi and the driver of the taxi was found and remembered the colonel. He says he took him to the train station to catch a train to Nice, and while he didn't see him actually board the train, he assumed he did so. Perret's notes say he believes the colonel to have left the area permanently, and to avoid an unpleasant scene didn't tell your mother he was leaving."

I stared at him and shook my head. "No, I cannot believe that. Captain Robillard, I assure you this is very much out of character for the colonel; he would not disappear without telling my mother first and he certainly would not leave her stranded at the dinner table, having made arrangements to meet her."

"Have you met the colonel, Miss Bridges?"

"Well no, but..."

"Then you cannot really speak as to his character?"

I stiffened automatically even though his tone was not in the least judgmental. "Perhaps not first hand, but my mother is an extremely good judge of character, Captain, and I believe her. You would too if you could speak to her. She's not one for melodrama and she is convinced something dreadful has happened."

"You do not believe then the Colonel is wooing another woman as well as your mother? It is quite common here. And incidentally it is what Perret believes."

"Certainly not, and Perret is mistaken. That may be the way of a Frenchman but it is not the way of the English. The colonel is a gentleman through and through."

"Not all Frenchmen, Miss Bridges," he replied with amusement. "And a man can be both a cad and a gentleman."

"Perhaps," I conceded, "but not in this case." I was wondering at his use of the word cad; his English really was excellent. I must have had the question in my eyes for he answered immediately.

"I studied at Oxford."

I nodded and smiled. I found I liked Captain Robillard but wasn't entirely sure I could trust him and I needed to be absolutely convinced before I told him I worked for Scotland Yard.

"You are thinking a great deal, Miss Bridges."

"Yes."

"If it makes you feel any easier I too do not feel your missing friend is at this moment in the arms of another woman in Nice. It is not usually the way of an Englishman as you say, but even less so that of a former colonel of the British army."

I let out a sigh of relief. "Then you'll help find him?"

"I will speak to Perret. I cannot promise you anything more than that but I will keep you informed. If perchance the colonel returns then please telephone me. Here is my card; it is my private number as I am not always to be found here."

I put the card in my bag and thanked him but the conversation had made me realise how little I knew about Colonel Summerfield.

"Captain Robillard, would you mind if I used your telephone? The one at the villa has been out of service and I have an urgent call to make."

"Of course, but I'm afraid I must leave you now as I have an appointment. Can you see yourself out?"

"Yes, thank you. Oh, Captain Robillard, there is just one other thing. My mother is of the opinion she is about to be arrested and I would like to put her mind at ease."

"Arrested? Why would she think that?"

"Because she was the last person to see Colonel Summerfield. Of course we know now that may not have been the case due to the witnesses, and also because she was his closest friend here."

"And who put this idea into her head? No, let me guess. Perret?"

I nodded. "I believe that may have been the case, yes."

"Well, you can assure her we have no intention of arresting her."

"Thank you, Captain."

He shook my hand and left closing the door behind him. I lifted the telephone receiver and put a call in to Sergeant Baxter. He came on the line a moment later, decidedly out of breath.

"Ello, Miss Bridges, you just caught me, practically out

the door. I didn't expect to hear from you. I thought you was in France?"

"I am, sergeant..."

"Actually it's Detective Sergeant now," he said with a note of pride in his voice.

"Oh, Baxter, you got the promotion. Congratulations, what wonderful news."

"Well, it was owing to that last case we worked on, Miss Bridges, so it's down to you really."

"Nonsense, I had little to do with it, it was on your own merit and well deserved if I may say so."

"P'raps. Now then, what can I do for you?"

I brought him up to date with what had been happening and I could hear him whistle in surprise.

"There's something happens everywhere you go. So you want to know all about the colonel? Do you know his regiment and all?"

I had obtained as much information as I could from my mother and dutifully passed it on to him, then gave the number at the villa for him to call me back.

"It's been out of order for a few days, I'm afraid but I think the one at the hotel is working if you can't get through."

"Righto, Miss Bridges, leave it with me."

"Thank you, Baxter. Goodbye."

"Cheerio."

I replaced the receiver and went back out into the main part of the station to find Belett replacing the receiver of the desk telephone. He smiled at me and said. "Au revoir, Mademoiselle." Then proceeded to a back office and shut the door.

※

As I stepped outside the police station into the warmth of the afternoon the bell on the town church rang the hour. Four o'clock, it was later than I thought. I walked to the end of the street and managed to find a taxi to take me back to the villa in time for tea.

I went straight out to the patio to find my mother and aunt already seated.

"Ella, darling, you're back. Don't worry about changing, come and sit down. How did you get on with the dreadful Perret?"

I took a seat and helped myself to the sandwiches. "Actually he wasn't there but I did speak to his superior, Captain Robillard." I took the card from my bag and handed it to her.

"Jacques Robillard, Capitaine." She handed it back to me and I slipped it back in my purse.

"What did the captain have to say?"

I told her the police had no intention of arresting her,

which brought immediate relief, then relayed the information about the witness statements. Both my aunt and mother were shocked.

"But, Ella, that can't be possible. I don't believe for a minute Edward would do such a thing."

"I agree, Elspeth," Aunt Margaret said.

"Well, perhaps Perret made the statements up so he didn't have to bother looking for Edward?"

"I honestly can't see that being the case mother. And we can't accuse a police official of falsifying evidence. Now, Let us suppose for argument's sake the statements are true..."

"Ella!"

"Listen a moment, mother. There is more than one way to interpret the information. When Edward left you that day he had plenty of time to do just what the statements suggest and get back in time for your dinner date. Perhaps he had brief business in Nice which we are unaware of?"

"But that would mean something happened to him either on the way to Nice or while he was there to prevent him returning."

"Exactly and personally I think that is the more likely. I doubt Perret would include witness statements which could so easily be disproved. As much as the man may be difficult and obnoxious, I don't think he is stupid enough to risk his career. He is undoubtedly lazy and a chauvinist to boot but sadly neither of those is a crime."

"But he also hasn't followed up on the statements. He should have gone to Nice and found further evidence of the colonel's arrival there," my aunt said, vigorously stirring her tea.

"Well of course he should, Margaret, but he was too focused on me being a nag and was convinced Edward had had enough of me and walked away. His incompetence is not only infuriating but could prove critical to Edward's wellbeing. Ella, what else did the captain say? Did he agree with the statements?"

"It was the first time he had seen them. He wasn't familiar with the case until I spoke with him."

"Well, that is decidedly odd," Aunt Margaret said. "Surely he would have reported back to his captain?"

"I agree, but Captain Robillard did mention to me he wasn't always at the police station, it could be Perret hasn't had chance as yet. Or as Perret believes nothing untoward has happened he may have felt it not worthwhile bothering his captain with. Regardless, Captain Robillard will be speaking with him in due course. However, he was in agreement that it sounded out of character for the colonel to disappear without informing you. He studied at Oxford so has obviously spent enough time in England to know the true countenance of an English gentleman. He's going to speak with Perret and will telephone me if there is news."

I had decided to keep back my telephone call to Baxter. Until I had some facts, I felt it would only upset my mother more to know I was garnering information on her friend. Not to mention the fact I wasn't entirely sure he was still alive.

"Well, that's something I suppose," mother said gloomily. "But it means we are no further forward and poor Edward could be suffering somewhere, or worse."

Yes, a lot worse I thought to myself. We were interrupted then by the ringing of the telephone bell.

"Madame, it was Madame Dubois. I am to say the parcel you are expecting will be here soon," said the maid.

"Thank you, Adele."

A moment later Adele returned. "Madame, Monsieur DuPont has just arrived."

The maid's poise was remarkable; there wasn't even the slightest muscle twitch to give the game away.

"Show him through, Adele, and please bring another setting and replenish the tea."

Pierre strutted onto the patio like a peacock, and not only that, he was dressed like one. A bright orange jacket was worn over a canary yellow shirt with a plum-coloured cravat at his neck. Lightweight trousers in lime green settled upon beach shoes in bright turquoise, above which a sliver of pink sock was evident. The entire ensemble was topped off by a multi-coloured embroidered fez with a gold tassel and a large blue and white beach umbrella. I wondered how on earth Adele had managed to keep a straight face, and Aunt Margaret nearly spat out her tea.

"Good god, Pierre!" she said, then was lost for words.

"You like?" he asked, giving a twirl. "I have found a new tailor."

"You don't say. Is he colour blind?"

Pierre scowled at my aunt and I couldn't help but laugh. It was just their way and he knew she meant nothing insulting.

"Take no notice, Pierre, I think you look splendid," my mother said. "Very bright and summery."

"Thank you, Elspeth. I knew immediately you were a woman of good taste."

"I thought we weren't drawing attention to ourselves?"

"Ah, Maggie, alas the entire Riviera knows I am here. It is a pointless exercise I feel."

As he helped himself to smoked salmon and cucumber sandwiches we brought him up to date about the witnesses.

He nodded solemnly. "Yes, it is true."

Three pairs of eyes swiveled toward him. "What do you mean it's true, Pierre?" my aunt asked.

"The colonel did go to Nice on the train. I spoke to a fellow guest at the hotel last evening, a man with mutton-chop whiskers, very unbecoming I thought."

"Major Dewberry," my mother said.

"Indeed it was. He plays an occasional game of bridge with your friend the colonel I believe?"

My mother nodded. "Yes. I don't play very well I'm afraid, but the major is an excellent player. They make up a foursome with an elderly married couple who live at the hotel."

"They were due to play the next evening," Pierre continued. "But Colonel Summerfield never arrived. The major was most put out about it, especially as he says he met the colonel at the train station and although he said he was on his way to Nice he confirmed he would be back that evening as he had a dinner date to keep. He also said he hadn't forgotten the game and was looking forward to the rematch."

"So Edward *did* go to Nice. Did the major say why he was going?"

"No, the conversation was but a brief one alas as the train was about to depart. However I also spoke with the manager and he says the colonel did not pack any of his belongings, but more importantly his passport is still in the hotel safe. It is therefore most definite in my mind that he intended to return."

❇

The remainder of tea was quite a subdued affair with us all lost in our own thoughts. I was of the opinion urgent inquiries regarding the colonel needed to be made in Nice, and intended to speak to Captain Robillard about it when he telephoned. I was also astounded at Perret's lack of investigation. It had been easy for Pierre to discover the colonel had left his passport and belongings at the hotel; it would have been just as easy for Perret to do the same, but he had done nothing. I sighed wondering if we were all just going through the motions. The description mother had given me of the colonel was so like the spirit on the aeroplane, perhaps we were already too late.

At just before six o'clock the maid announced the expected delivery had arrived.

"Oh yes, the paintings, I had quite forgotten they were due."

"Paintings?" asked Pierre, his eyes alight with interest.

"Mother has done Aunt Margaret and me an oil each as a gift, Pierre. They really are jolly good too."

"Might I be permitted to see them, Elspeth?"

"Of course, but don't expect too much, Pierre, I am just an enthusiastic amateur. Adele, please bring the parcel through."

"My dear Madame, you have been hiding your light beneath a bushel," Pierre exclaimed after carefully unwrapping the canvasses.

My mother blushed quite becomingly. "Thank you for your kind words but they are nothing compared to your professional standard."

"Of course not, you are not a professional artiste, but you have a good eye for composition and some genuine talent. May I take them back to the hotel with me I would like to study them properly?"

"By all means. I'll have Adele parcel them up for you." She rang the small hand bell and the maid appeared at once. "Adele, please pack the art school paintings. Monsieur DuPont wishes to take them with him."

She took the proffered artwork from Pierre and he said, "You can give them to my driver Gaston. He is waiting outside."

"Oui, monsieur."

"And, Elspeth," Pierre continued, "I have the most perfect little gift for you at my gallery. I shall telephone to Hilda asking her to send it on."

Aunt Margaret and I shared a knowing glance. Pierre had a truly uncanny ability to choose a painting perfectly suited to the person, even though he may have just met them and the painting concerned done years prior. He'd already furnished me and Baxter, who was a fan, with exceptional pieces during our last investigation. I wondered what he would choose for my mother.

"Tell her not to use the post, Pierre," said Aunt Margaret. "Apparently several of the pieces done by the amateur students at the school have never arrived."

"Is that so? How interesting. Well, perhaps I shall find another way. Now it is time for me to bid you all adieu but first the reason for my visit." He reached into an inner pocket of his jacket and produced three envelopes, handing one to each of us.

"Eh voilá! Invitations to the opening of the new show at Galerie Tuel tomorrow evening, a most prestigious affair."

"Oh, Pierre, how wonderful," my mother said, and my aunt and I agreed. From what I understood these invitations were terribly difficult to obtain and were only given to the most distinguished of guests. Pierre strutted away humming a jaunty little tune, with promises to send his driver for us.

"Well, it seems we have arrived," Aunt Margaret said, a wry smile on her face. "So much for keeping a low profile."

※

As we moved indoors the telephone bell could be heard ringing in the hall and shortly after the maid announced it was Captain Robillard for me.

"Captain Robillard, good evening."

"Good evening, Miss Bridges. I am ringing to inform you I spoke with Lieutenant Perret an hour ago and he stands by the statements. He is also still of the opinion the colonel was meeting with a lady friend."

"As a matter of fact I have just had confirmation this evening that Colonel Summerfield did take the train to Nice. However, his intention was most assuredly to return, which he did not."

I quickly recounted the conversation with Pierre.

"I see."

"Do you really, Captain? To my mind it's most suspicious that Colonel Summerfield would leave all his belongings, including his passport, at the hotel. If his intention was to leave my mother for another woman then I believe he would make a clean breast of it and move out of the hotel completely. The risk of him bumping into her whenever he decided to return and the ensuing embarrassment would be too great. It's a small expatriate community here, Captain, as I'm sure you know."

"You make a good case, Miss Bridges, and as I said at our meeting it does seem to be out of character for the colonel."

"Captain, I feel sure something happened to Edward Summerfield either en route to, or in Nice. Could you make some inquiries to find out his movements from when the major spoke with him at the train station? The longer he is missing the more concerned I am for his welfare."

There was a pause before he spoke again. "Miss Bridges, before I agree to anything perhaps you can answer a question?"

"Yes?"

"Just what is your connection to Scotland Yard?"

So Belett the weasel had lived up to his name. Not only had he listened in to my private conversation, but as I surmised he also understood every word. I felt the heat flush my face as the anger took hold and took a deep breath to calm down; it would do no good to get angry. I wondered if the captain had given Belett those exact instructions before he left? And found myself feeling disappointed at the possibility.

I said through gritted teeth, "I'm sure Belett can give you a detailed account of the conversation, Captain Robillard..."

"I have no wish to offend you, Miss Bridges, and Belett has been suitably reprimanded for his actions, however I cannot forget that which I am told whatever the source. If I am to help you then I would prefer to start with us both being on the level."

The anger disappeared as quickly as it had come and I found myself smiling at his gentle tone and rational words, "You make a good case yourself, Captain Robillard. I am in fact a consultant detective with Scotland Yard and work closely with Detective Sergeant Baxter. As you are no doubt aware it was Baxter I telephoned from your office. It occurred to me how little I knew about the colonel, and in light of what has happened felt it prudent to rectify that. Baxter is looking into his background for me. I also work with Police Commissioner Montesford on occasion; he is godfather to my sister-in-law and the one who originally spoke to the Home Secretary to put me forward for the position. This isn't in any way an official visit. I am purely here at my mother's request. So will you help?"

He laughed softly. "It would seem the most sensible course of action if I want to avoid an international incident."

"Thank you, Captain. Will you let me know when there is news?"

"Naturally. Could you also share what you learn from your detective friend?"

"In the spirit of international relations?"

"Something like that, Miss Bridges."

I laughed. "Of course I will. Goodnight, Captain Robillard."

"Bonne nuit, Miss Bridges."

Back in the sitting room I announced that further inquiries were now being made in Nice, and that Captain Robillard and myself were liaising directly as he was now aware of my connection to Scotland Yard.

"Is he sending Perret?" my mother asked.

"He didn't say who he was sending but I have the feeling it will not be Perret. I don't believe he was particularly impressed with the work he has done so far."

After a pleasant dinner we agreed to retire early. With little more we could do on the case we had decided a day at the beach was in order, followed by the gallery show in the evening. However, while the day-trip was wonderful, that night was to be an event none of us would ever forget, and for all the wrong reasons.

Chapter SIX

THE NEXT MORNING I AWOKE feeling fully rested and ready for the day's excursions. I had expected to have a restless night with the worry of the case, but Phantom had visited and I felt sure he was the reason I had calmed.

I had been reading when I noticed a familiar black shape jump onto the end of the bed and work its way up to my knees where it settled on my lap. "Hello dear cat," I'd said, and was rewarded with an aristocratic gaze which I'd come to realise is a characteristic of all cats, whether they are of the ghostly kind or not. He was solid too, which was a rarity, and although silent I could feel his purr reverberate under my hand as I gently stroked his sleek fur.

I'd talked to him for a while, putting my thoughts in order, then turning out the lamp drifted off to sleep with him curled up beside me. When I awoke he had gone.

Now I rose and drew back the curtains to another glorious day. I adored Linhay Island and my home tremendously, but there was something very satisfying about waking up and knowing it would be sunny and warm. In England, good weather was never guaranteed.

When I had left them the day before to visit the police station, my mother and aunt had taken the opportunity to go shopping and they had bought me a gift. I opened the box now and took out the one-piece swimming costume in navy blue with red and white trim. It came with a matching blue swim cap with white polka dots and a white sleeveless beach gown with a blue and red tie belt. It was the latest fashion, fit like a glove and I was absolutely thrilled with it.

Mother had arranged a picnic lunch and mid morning, after we had let our leisurely breakfast settle, we set off down the private steps to the beach.

Sun beds had been set out and parasols already erected by my mother's butler so it was just a case of getting settled. Unlike the pebble and shingle beach at Linhay, this one was of the softest finest sand I had ever seen and was a joy to walk on in bare feet.

"I'm going for a swim. Is anyone going to join me?"

"I will," my mother said. "I try and swim everyday if I can and have missed it recently."

"It's a long time since I've swum in an azure sea and

I intend to make the most of it while I am here, and before my body decides enough is enough," my aunt said.

So the three of us walked down the beach together, enjoying the warmth of the sun on our skin and the soft sand between our toes. The water was heavenly, the waves gentle, and we swam and bobbed about, floating on our backs and chatting and laughing and splashing for a long while before returning to our sun beds and relaxing.

"So tell me about Captain Robillard, Ella," my mother suddenly said. "Is he handsome? What age is he?"

"Mother!"

She laughed gaily and I found myself joining in.

"They are just questions, dear, I'm interested."

"You're not being in the least bit subtle, Elspeth," my aunt said from beneath the sun hat perched on her nose. I had thought she was asleep.

"There's no need for subtly when it's family. I just feel if he is working with Ella to help find Edward then I'd like to know more about him."

"And will his being handsome or not allow him to do his job better or worse, do you think?"

"Oh, Margaret," mother said, laughing. "All right I could have been a little less obvious but I still would like to know. Ella came back with a lovely flush after that telephone call last night."

"Yes, I agree with that."

"Well really!" I said. "You do realise I'm just sitting here, don't you?"

This produced mirth from both sisters.

"Of course we do, darling, I'm just teasing."

But I could tell she was still waiting for me to answer; in fact they both were and I would get no peace until I did so.

"Well, if you really want to know, I would say he is in his early thirties. I don't know if he's married or not. There was no wedding band but that's quite common nowadays, and yes he is handsome. He also seems to be good at his job and I feel I can trust him." At that moment Adele came walking over to us with the picnic basket.

"Saved by the maid," my aunt whispered and gave me a wink.

The swimming and fresh air had made me ravenous and the roast chicken and salad, accompanied by iced tea and homemade lemonade and finished off with a fruit sorbet, tasted like the food of the gods. Adele came and cleared away the detritus and the afternoon was spent with more swimming and walks along the sand. I strolled along the wooden jetty and sat at the end beneath my red parasol with my toes dipped in the water, and thought how peaceful and relaxing it all was. It was a perfect day and I was very glad I had made the most of it for it was to be my last for a while.

❋

I was just putting the finishing touches to my evening dress when there was a tap at my door, "Come in."

"It's only me, darling, oh what a gorgeous gown."

It was the one my sister-in-law Ginny had persuaded me to buy for the dinner party up at Arundel Hall several months ago. I'd only worn it the once and I'd forgotten how flattering and comfortable it was, if a little risqué. But here on the Riviera and particularly for this evening's soirée it was most suitable.

"As is yours, mother, you look beautiful."

Her gown was a flowing skirt in silk and chiffon, turquoise in colour with a tight bodice to show off her perfect figure and elbow length sleeves. The whole was set off perfectly with discreet diamond jewellery.

"I've brought you this; I thought you might like to wear it this evening."

She handed me a beautiful hair comb in silver decorated with diamonds and pearls. It was a perfect match to the earrings and necklace I was wearing.

"Sit down and I'll do your hair for you."

I was perfectly capable of roughly pinning up my hair but the sleek chignon my mother deftly produced was beyond me.

"The telephone is working again and I've just had a lovely conversation with Jerry and Ginny," she told me as she affixed the comb.

"How are they both? Is Ginny feeling a bit better?"

"I believe she is a little, although it can go on for some time. I felt dreadfully sick with both of you almost to the end. Then again I had a friend who never felt ill at all so you can never tell. They are both terribly excited about it and I've told them they can expect me nearer the time. It looks as though we will all be descending on you for Christmas."

"Oh I would love it, Mother. I've wanted to dress the large dining room for Christmas ever since I discovered it behind the secret panel, and with a brand new addition to the family it will be even more special."

Another knock at the door and Aunt Margaret entered.

"The car is here, my dears, are we ready?"

"Aunt Margaret, you look wonderful."

Her dress was similar to my mothers, but in a deep green satin with gold accents and sparkling emerald jewellery.

"One does one's best you know," she said, patting her hair comically and striking a pose. "And I must say the two of you look dazzling, very elegant indeed. I hope there's a photographer present; we should have our picture taken; I doubt we'll be dressed like this again for a while. Come along then, we had best not leave Gaston waiting."

"Is Pierre here?"

"No he's gone on ahead and will meet us there. Apparently he doesn't want to overshadow our entrance," Aunt Margaret said rolling her eyes.

Galerie Tuel was already full of guests when we arrived and were ushered into the building by the large doorman. A few heads from small groups turned to look when we entered, but either turned away again somewhat dismissively, or frowned as though trying to place us.

"We're obviously not famous enough," my aunt said in amusement.

A waiter approached with a tray of champagne flutes followed closely by another offering hors d'oeuvres, and having partaken of both we wandered into the main room. It was a beautiful space lit up with several sparkling chandeliers and strategically placed wall and table lamps, showing off paintings and sculptures.

The rear section was cordoned off with a deep red rope and beyond I saw several easels covered with swathes of fabric that reached the floor. This was obviously the main display and the reason for the gala. A photographer with an assistant, hired for the evening by the gallery, was taking portraits of the guests, his flash bulb popping audibly every few minutes, and we three posed for one together. My mother gave him her card and asked that he send her three copies, to which he agreed.

"What a sight to behold. Can it be Aphrodite and her daughters?"

We turned to find Pierre in shades of yellow and pink twinkling up at us.

"Oh do be sensible, Pierre," my aunt said. "For one thing I am not old enough to be Elspeth's mother, and for another we have far too many clothes on. Now why are you dressed as a dolly mixture?"

My mother looked at me in semi shocked amusement; she still wasn't used to their teasing. I on the other hand couldn't contain my laughter.

"Oh, you know how to wound a man with your sharp tongue, Maggie," and as if to demonstrate his meaning he clutched at his heart and staggered two steps back. "It was a compliment, my dear woman."

"Well a simple, 'you all look positively divine this evening ladies,' would have sufficed. Now you're drawing attention to us."

I looked around to see she was right. Several people were glancing our way, some with indulgent smiles at the antics of 'the little man,' others laughing along with him. I caught the eye of a stunning almost ethereal young couple who glanced at each other, then away, obviously embarrassed to be caught staring, and an elderly lady dressed much as Queen Victoria would have done had she been here, whose expression said, 'we are not amused.' I also caught sight of the art teacher Valin but he was not looking in our direction thankfully. Pierre didn't care a jot.

"Pah! Let them stare."

We were saved further scrutiny when a voice called over

the hubbub, announcing the unveiling. Pierre offered my aunt his arm which made her laugh as it was down near her right hip. Jokingly she rested her hand on his head instead, he chuckled, and removing it they walked in side-by-side. The crowd moved as one toward the end of the room where the rope had been removed, and we found ourselves at the front of the throng. As the gallery owner began his short speech I spied the attractive couple at the end of the front row to my right. I could hear the speech coming to an end but my eyes were still on the couple. Her dress was sensational and I was wondering where it was from.

Suddenly she flinched, her hand tightened on the arm of her companion and she turned away, revealing a rose-coloured birthmark on her shoulder. A split second later an earsplitting scream filled the silence.

※

My mother clutched my arm tightly and swayed. I looked at the unveiled easel and saw, crammed at an unnatural angle beneath the three wooden legs, the body of a woman and it was obvious she was dead. I glanced back but the couple had gone. Then chaos broke out as further screams sounded, several women fainted and the remaining crowd moved hurriedly en masse toward the exit, crushing those who were either too slow or too dazed. I handed mother over to my aunt who, although sickly pale, was upright, then grabbed Pierre.

"Pierre, quickly: go and lock the gallery doors. No one must leave." A flash bulb popped somewhere over my shoulder. "And confiscate that camera!"

He nodded and hurried away. Next I approached the owner who was leaning against a wall on the verge of fainting.

"Monsieur Tuel?" He stared at me with no comprehension. I tried again. "Are you the owner, Monsieur Tuel?"

"Oui... er, yes I am Tuel."

"Monsieur Tuel, listen to me. You must ring the police at once and ask for Captain Robillard. Here is his card." I fished it out of my bag and handed it to him. "Do you understand? You need to telephone. Now!"

Thankfully he seemed to come round at the sense of urgency in my voice.

"Yes, I understand, I will do it now."

"Please hurry, Monsieur Tuel."

As he left I approached the body. Someone had had the foresight to reinstate the rope and the guests had been ushered to the other side. My intention was to replace the fabric cover and I did so, but not before I had seen who was underneath. I gasped in shock. It had been impossible to identify before due to the angle but now I could see her face, I recognised her immediately. It was Clementine Dubois.

Above the shock and profound sadness for a woman I barely knew but had liked immediately, I forced myself to be objective. Blocking out the sounds of hysteria from the room behind, I quickly absorbed as much of the detail as I could before replacing the fabric throw and joining the rest of the crowd in the main room.

What I had seen didn't make sense and to my mind was suspicious; I needed to speak to Jacques Robillard. But first I needed to break the news to my mother before anyone else did.

I found her seated in a small antechamber to the side of the entrance with my aunt. No doubt Pierre had arranged that and I was terribly grateful. I spied him at the door with Monsieur Tuel both deep in conversation while they waited for the authorities. I was gratified to see the doorman had taken possession of the camera and was taking the guarding of it most seriously. I also noticed the photographer slumped in a chair with an ice pack on an already swelling eye.

I stepped into the tiny room and, hunching before her chair, took my mother's hands.

"How are you feeling?"

"I'm all right, Ella, it was just such a shock. What a terrible thing to happen. Who is it, do you know?"

I glanced at my aunt who raised a quizzical eyebrow, my mother saw the exchange.

"What is it? Do you know who it is?"

"Darling, I'm so sorry, I'm afraid it's Clementine Dubois."

"Clementine? No, no, that can't be right. I didn't know she was coming. She would have told me if she was attending."

"I don't think she was invited."

"What do you mean, Ella? Are you sure it's her? You only met her recently, you could be mistaken?"

"I'm sure, mother. I'm so sorry," I enveloped her in a hug as she gently wept on my shoulder. I looked at my aunt and asked if she was all right.

"Yes, don't worry about me, dear, but I really think we should get Elspeth home."

"I'll see what I can do when Captain Robillard appears. There will be formal statements and such but we can do those just as well back at the villa."

"I think he's just arrived."

I turned my head to peer through the archway to the room beyond and saw the captain speaking with Monsieur Tuel and Pierre while his men spanned the room. He glanced over and his eyes widened slightly as he saw me.

"Mother, will you be all right if I go and speak to the police?"

She nodded while dabbing her eyes with her handkerchief, "I'll be fine, Ella, Margaret's here and when the initial shock has worn off a little... go and do your job, darling."

I squeezed her shoulder, smiled at my aunt and went to join the captain.

Chapter SEVEN

※

I WAITED WHILE Robillard finished his conversation and instructed his men to take control of the room. He also organised the waiters to bring water and coffee to those who needed it. As the police began to take details from the guests I glanced to the end of the room where the body lay, and saw two officers struggling with a temporary screen. They at last managed to erect it, successfully shielding the sight from onlookers, and I watched as the captain beckoned toward a thin, pale man with thick lensed spectacles, who had been patiently waiting at the entrance. He carried a doctor's bag. This then was the French equivalent of a pathologist here to scrutinise the scene. Robillard escorted him to the far end of the gallery, all the while in deep conversation, and then returned to me.

"Miss Bridges, I didn't expect to see you here."

"Nor I you, Captain."

He took my elbow and expertly steered me across the room, "Perhaps we could talk privately. I have the use of Tuel's office."

The office was up a private staircase to the rear of a mezzanine floor, with a balcony overlooking the entire room below. I took a moment to scan the crowd but didn't see what I was looking for, which confirmed the notion I had had earlier. I went to join Robillard in the well appointed and comfortable office, putting my thoughts in order as I went.

"Now, what can you tell me about the events of the evening? I have just been speaking to Monsieur Tuel and Monsieur DuPont, I believe it was you who ordered the door locked and asked Monsieur Tuel to telephone me?"

"Yes. Fortunately I still had your card in my purse."

He took out another and slid it across the mirrored table toward me. I put it in my purse, replacing the one I had given away.

"There are numerous high level dignitaries here this evening, Miss Bridges, and I guarantee within half an hour once the shock has worn off there will be a stampede to the door. I would like to have your observations before that happens."

"Of course, but I would like to request a favour, if I may? My mother is terribly upset and I feel she would be better at home. I wonder if you would allow my aunt and her to leave? They would of course be available whenever you need them to give a statement."

"There are many upset people here. Why should I favour your mother?"

I bristled slightly but his words were spoken gently. "Because the victim was a friend of hers. I'm afraid I had to tell her before..."

"Stop, please. You mean to say you know who the victim is?"

"Yes. I didn't at first but I took the liberty of replacing the cloth over the easel and recognised her then. Do you know the cause of death?"

"Not at the moment. We will not know for certain until the autopsy. Now who was she?"

"Her name is, was, Clementine Dubois. She ran the art school just outside the grounds of the hotel where my mother's villa is."

"I see, and you knew her well?"

"No, I only met her the day before yesterday when we went for a tour round. Mother and Colonel Summerfield have been taking classes."

"Colonel Summerfield?"

"Yes. Mother had done a couple of paintings as a gift for my aunt and I and she wanted to show them to us."

"And this is the only reason you visited the school? For a tour and to look at your mother's art?"

I paused only briefly but it was still too long for the captain and he pounced immediately.

"I see. You were investigating the colonel's disappearance?"

"It's why I came, Captain Robillard. My mother requested my help."

"And this was the same day you came to see me, yes?"

I nodded. He had been taking notes during our entire conversation, and I waited while he caught up.

"Now about this evening, is there anything you noticed which may help me?"

"As a matter of fact there was."

I began with our arrival and the appearance of Pierre at our side; omitting the private jokes between him and my aunt I mentioned that his greeting of us drew attention.

"He's very well known of course and I think many guests were wondering who we were that we should garner such favouritism. However, when I glanced up I caught the eye of a stunning young couple at the side of the room. They turned away when I saw they were looking and initially I thought it was embarrassment."

"Understandable."

"Precisely, but then the unveiling was announced. We were right at the front of the spectators as were this couple; they had a position almost at the end of the first row to my right and just as Monsieur Tuel was to remove the cover, the girl flinched, gripped her partner's arm and looked away."

"It was a devastating sight, a dead body under the easel. I'm sure many people flinched."

"No, you don't understand. The girl flinched and looked away just before the unveiling. Captain Robillard, she knew exactly what would be underneath that cloth."

"Mon Dieu!" Robillard exploded. "You are sure?"

"I am positive, Captain."

He half rose, saying, "Well, point them out to me at once."

I shook my head. "They are no longer here..."

"But the door was locked. You arranged it yourself. How could they leave?"

"As soon as the first scream went up I naturally looked away to see what had caused it, but it was just a second later that I looked back and they were gone. It is my guess they left in the ensuing chaos before Pierre locked the door. No one would have taken any notice at that point. I also looked down at the room over the balcony to see if I could see them before you and I came in here. They were not there."

He ran a frustrated hand through his dark hair, causing it to stand up. "I don't suppose you knew who they were?"

"I'm sorry, no. Perhaps other guests recognise them? Pierre maybe? He seems to know everyone. Or Monsieur Tuel? They would have needed an invitation to have been present."

"Yes, all this crossed my mind also. Can you describe them for me, please?"

I closed my eyes to better recall the details in my mind.

"They were both slim with such light hair as to be almost white. Hers was pinned up but with loose tendrils to just below her shoulders, his was short and swept straight back. Both had pale skin with light-coloured eyes, possibly blue or grey but I was never close enough to see properly. He had a small beard and moustache, a goatee, if you understand the word?" I said, opening my eyes for a moment.

He nodded while he wrote. I closed my eyes again.

"The beard was the same colour as his hair. I would estimate her to be approximately my height while he was nearer six foot. She wore a sleeveless dress gathered at the shoulders with diamond brooches, in a shimmering light silk, grey green one moment but as she moved it changed colour to violet and silver. It reminded me of a waterfall catching moonlight, quite mesmerising. The man's jacket and cummerbund were of the same fabric, as was his bow tie. His trousers and shirt were of dark grey and shoes black. They had definitely dressed to match, but they both looked almost ethereal as though they weren't quite real."

"Well, I hope for our sake they were. Anything else?"

"I think they were related by blood in some way as opposed to by marriage."

"Siblings perhaps?"

"Yes or maybe first cousins. Their features were too similar to be otherwise. That's all I can tell you, although the photographer may have got a picture of them."

"Merci, you have an excellent eye for detail."

"I practice continually. In our profession it pays to have a good eye. But in all honesty if they hadn't have been quite so unusually striking, I wouldn't have remembered as much as I have."

He nodded and smiled. "Excuse me a moment while I update my men."

He was back a few minutes later.

"The guests are now being questioned about this couple as is Monsieur Tuel and the photographer. The guest list is being checked off against the guests who are still here and if all goes well we should have a name shortly. Is there anything else you can tell me before I accompany you and your family home?"

"You are coming back to the villa with us?"

"I am. I would like to speak to your mother as she knew the victim well and her information could be invaluable. I also think it would be better to interview her in the comfort of her own home to avoid any more stress. I've told my men I will be interviewing her personally so she will be left alone, as will your aunt."

"Thank you, Captain Robillard, I appreciate it. There

was one other thing: I don't believe Clementine Dubois had been invited to this event."

"We will check the guest list but what makes you say that?"

"I met her, remember, and she struck me at the time as the epitome of French chic. Everything about her shouted taste and style and up to the minute fashion, and this was one of the most talked about events of the year. Invitations were worth their weight in gold and incredibly rare. We are only here due to Pierre's celebrity. My mother will confirm but I don't think Clementine Dubois was in such straitened circumstances as to wear a gown at least three seasons out of date, which was two sizes too big for her. Shoes which taste decrees should never have been paired with the dress and rather tellingly were too small, and paste jewellery. This was not so much about the art but a place to see and be seen and Clementine Dubois would not have been seen dressed as she was. And as a friend she most likely would have told my mother had she been invited, and she didn't."

"You know a lot about fashion, I see."

I smiled. "If you had asked me that question a few months ago I would have laughed. I couldn't have told you the difference between a Chanel and a cabbage and quite often went out wearing odd shoes. I was better educated due to an assignment I was asked to consult on very briefly in between my normal cases. An exclusive clothing boutique in London was convinced their designs were being stolen and copies sold cheaply. Their concerns were well founded. The culprit has since been arrested and the enterprise closed down but I learned about the fashion industry while I was involved."

"Well, don't let Madame Coco hear you compare her clothing to cabbages, she has a house here you know." He leant back and sighed deeply. "But why would Madame Dubois dress in such a way? Or are you saying someone else dressed her like this?"

I shrugged. "Either is possible but it may be more likely that she was forced to dress as she did?"

"But why?"

"I don't know. But it's my considered opinion that the whole thing was staged and was done to send a message to someone."

❋

As we waited in the warmth of the evening for Captain Robillard to bring his car around, Pierre informed us he would make his own way back to the hotel; he wanted to spend a little more time with Monsieur Tuel who was beside himself with worry.

My mother had rallied somewhat thanks to my aunt, but of course was feeling the loss of her friend greatly. It was a mere two minutes before the captain pulled up in front of the gallery where we were waiting.

"Good heavens!" my aunt exclaimed eyeing the long, open top sleek sports car in dual tones of café-au-lait and whipped cream.

Captain Robillard jumped out of the driver's side. "I apologise, ladies, it may be a little cramped but the journey is not a long one. Tuel telephoned to my private number and I was naturally at home so had to bring my own car." He levered forward the two front seats and we climbed, a tad awkwardly, into the rear. It was indeed a little cramped but we managed. Robillard hopped back in the driver's seat with a police constable at his side and we pulled out into the traffic.

The journey wasn't at all long and the captain drove quite sedately. However, we certainly arrived back at mother's villa decidedly more windswept than we had left it.

"Well, that's odd," my mother said when we pulled through the gates. "The light above the door is out."

"Perhaps the staff forgot to change the bulb?" I said.

"Well, it will be the first time if that's the case."

"Are your staff in the house, Madame Bridges?"

"No, Captain, I gave them both the night off as we were to be out. My cook doesn't live in."

It was almost pitch black outside the villa and the voices came as though disembodied through the dark.

"Please wait here, ladies, I have a torch."

A moment later a shaft of light lit up the ground and we watched the captain's feet march up the steps. The crunch of broken glass as he reached the top was unmistakable.

"Madame Bridges, please give your keys to my officer."

"Yes, of course. She fumbled blindly in her bag and did as she was asked; the officer then proceeded to the captain aided by the torchlight.

In was an interminable length of time before captain Robillard returned. The villa was now lit up like a Christmas tree and we could see some of the mess through the open door as he descended the steps towards us.

"Madame Bridges, I am sorry to inform you that you have been burgled."

My mother slumped against the car. "Burgled? But why on earth should anyone want to burgle me?"

"How did they get in, Captain, when the door was locked at this side?" I asked.

"They broke through a window into the servant's quarters and entered the main house via the staff staircase. They are no longer here but I am afraid things are quite a mess. Mrs Bridges, do you feel up to coming in and seeing if anything is missing?"

"Of course. No one is going to keep me out of my own home. How dare they do this to me! Well this is the final straw. I shall take no more of this nonsense."

"Well said, Elspeth. We're British and they have no idea who they are dealing with," my aunt said as they both followed the constable indoors.

"And they look so soft on the outside," Robillard murmured next to me.

I laughed. "Never underestimate the strength of a woman, Captain, especially a British one."

"I would not dare," then, "I like them. They remind me of my own mother."

"She is British?"

"Was. She died when I was quite young."

"I'm sorry."

I felt rather than saw him shrug. "It was a long time ago. Now what do you think of all this?"

"It can't be a coincidence," I said. "First Colonel Summerfield goes missing, then Clementine Dubois is murdered and my mother is burgled on the same night. Somebody knew we were to be out and the house would be empty. I think it is all connected somehow."

"I agree. I have been through the house and it is not all thrown about in a haphazard way as you would expect from a simple burglary, one where they would take everything and anything of value quickly and with no thought to the mess. Each room has been systematically searched including the bathrooms. The staff quarters have not been touched at all. A jewellery box in one of the dressing rooms is open but the contents remain. No, whoever is responsible was looking for something specific. Do you have any idea what that could be?"

"You have no idea how much I want to say yes, Captain Robillard. However, I am completely baffled."

"Well, I have called my men from your mother's telephone. They will be here shortly. Possibly they will find something of use, fingerprints perhaps to lead us to the culprits. In the meantime I would suggest you all collect what you will need for an overnight stay at the hotel. I took the liberty of telephoning Monsieur DuPont and he has invited you to use his suite."

I nodded wearily. Suddenly the events of the last few hours caught up with me and I felt exhausted. "What about the staff? I should think they will return soon."

"I will deal with the staff, Miss Bridges, if they return."

"If? Do you think they are involved?"

"I don't think one way or the other, Miss Bridges. It is simply good police work to look at all those involved."

I decided to let the mild rebuke slide. "Is there any news about Colonel Summerfield as yet?"

"No. As far as the investigation goes it is as though he has disappeared into thin air."

※

With arrangements made for Captain Robillard to meet us the next morning we were escorted into the hotel's birdcage lift by the operator, and delivered to Pierre's suite just moments before the bellhop arrived with our cases.

The suite was palatial, consisting of two bedrooms with adjacent dressing rooms and bathrooms, and a spacious lounge. Aunt Margaret and my mother were sharing the larger room, I was in the smaller and Pierre had had the management set up a temporary bed in his dressing room, which he assured us was perfectly fine.

"I have slept in far worse places, my dears."

The events of the last few days, coming as they had one after the other, had exhausted us all, so we agreed it was best we retire at once, hopefully we would awake the following morning refreshed and ready for what the day would bring. It was as I was drifting off, floating in the space between deep sleep and not quite awake, I realised I had forgotten to tell the captain about the birthmark, and when I awoke it had once again slipped my mind.

It had been dark when I had gone to bed, and when a knock at the door and a voice informing me breakfast was imminent forced me to open my eyes, the sun was streaming in through the curtains. It felt as though only five minutes had passed since I'd closed my eyes. I groaned and answered, then forced myself to get up.

When I entered the lounge I saw breakfast had been delivered along with several newspapers and my mother and aunt were already seated. They looked as tired and drawn as I felt.

"Good morning," I said, bending to give them each a light kiss. "How did you sleep?"

"I went out like a light. I'd expected to be awake for hours."

"Emotional fatigue, Elspeth, I expect we were all the same."

"Where's Pierre?" I asked, helping myself to croissants and coffee.

"Visiting Monsieur Tuel. I see the papers are full of last night's events; it's remarkable how quickly they can produce a story. Luckily we aren't in it."

"May I see?" Aunt Margaret handed me her newspaper and I saw the news had made the headlines and spread to several pages inside. It was all in French so I couldn't understand it, but there were pictures of the guests.

"Thank goodness that photographer had his camera confiscated," my aunt said. "I dread to think what the front page would look like otherwise."

I glanced up at her. "How could they have pictures if there was no camera?"

"Good point. But he had an assistant, didn't he? Perhaps he had them?"

"Do you know, Aunt Margaret, I didn't see the assistant after the doors were locked. I suspect once the photographer realised this would be a huge story he had him hot foot it out of there with the film and straight round to the newspaper offices."

"Typical press," my mother remarked in disgust.

Having fully perused the front page, I turned to the inside pages where a photograph immediately caught my eye. "Oh!"

"What is it, Ella?"

"This photograph," I said pointing.

My mother looked and said, "Oh yes, they're very famous, part of a banking dynasty, but why are they important?"

"No, I don't mean them. Look at the couple behind them who have been inadvertently caught in the picture."

"What a striking looking pair," my aunt said.

It was the ethereal couple I had observed. Unfortunately there was no name listed as they had been caught unawares.

"Mother, do you recognise them?"

"I'm afraid I don't, darling. Why are they important?"

I explained to them both what I had seen the night before.

"They knew what was going to happen? I don't know what to say. How simply dreadful," mother exclaimed.

"I assume you told Captain Robillard all this?"

"Of course, Aunt Margaret. We need to find out who they are and go and speak to them at once."

"Well, that's a job for the police surely?" my mother asked.

I looked at her and smiled.

"Sorry, darling, just ignore me. I'm tired."

"Captain Robillard should be here any minute now. I'll show him then."

"I wonder what news he'll have of the burglary."

Chapter EIGHT

※

NO MORE THAN TEN MINUTES after the breakfast had been cleared, there was a knock at the door and Captain Robillard entered. He had washed and changed but there was an underlying fatigue which made me wonder if he had slept at all.

"Bonjour, ladies, my apologies for the early call but there is much to get through today."

"We understand, Captain. Can I get you coffee before you start?"

"No, thank you, Miss Bridges."

"Then let's go through to the lounge where it's comfortable."

Once we were all seated, Robillard began.

"If I may first go back to the events at your villa last evening, Madame Bridges, you indicated to me there was nothing you could see missing, yes?"

"Well, it was all a dreadful shock, especially after what had happened at the art show, but to the best of my knowledge nothing had been stolen"

"Of course. Your maid and your butler returned last night and both were naturally upset at what had happened. However, I believe neither of them were involved as their movements have been accounted for. Your maid also confirmed she could see nothing missing. Now it seems you have no alarm for the villa, may I ask why?"

"There never has been one as far as I know and I've never seen a need until now. It is supposed to be a very safe and secure environment, Captain, being as it is in the hotel grounds. The community is a gated one with security staff, and exclusive; the residents of both the hotel and the private villas are not of the criminal sort."

"You do not think the rich, the titled and the famous have a criminal element, Madame Bridges?" Captain Robillard said with a note of irony.

"I'm sure they do, Captain, but not here. It's rather grubby to break in to the home of one's neighbor, don't you think?

He smiled. "And the staff?"

"All the staff undergo exhaustive checks into their background by the management prior to being employed."

"It certainly makes one wonder how these thieves got past all that, doesn't it?" my aunt remarked.

Captain Robillard nodded. "We have already questioned the security guards, and apart from the police and those whose identities have been confirmed, no one else passed through any of the gates. But of course we will continue to pursue the matter. Now perhaps, Madame Bridges, you could tell me about your friend Clementine Dubois? I realise it is a difficult subject but anything you can tell me will help."

There was nothing my aunt or me could add to this part of the interview, so we remained silent while my mother told the captain all she could about her friend. It was difficult for her and she faltered with emotion more than once but she held together and eventually came to our art school visit.

"Then as we were walking out we heard Monsieur Valin in a rather heated conversation on the telephone."

Robillard perked up. "Oh?"

"Yes, I don't know who he was speaking with but he was very angry."

"Can you remember what he said?"

"Yes I think so. He said how impossible it was to do his job while Clementine insisted on showing all and sundry around while he was teaching. He was furious she had undermined his authority after he had already said no to us looking in the small gallery-cum-storeroom where my paintings were. He accused her of interfering and threatened to leave his job unless something was done about her..." she tailed off as what she just said dawned on her. "Oh, Captain, it's all my fault. We should never have gone. It must have made Valin so angry that he killed her."

"I agree it is quite a damning conversation in light of what has happened, Madame Bridges, but rest assured it was not your fault. Valin only threatened to leave his teaching position, he did not threaten to hurt Madame Dubois. Please do not blame yourself. I will make arrangements to speak to Valin as soon as possible."

"Has someone not already done so?" I asked. "I saw him at the gallery last night."

"Pardon? Are you sure?"

"Positive."

Robillard paged back in his notebook and eventually found what he was looking for. "Mon dieu! There was never an interview with him but he was on the guest list. This means he also must have slipped out!"

At that moment the telephone bell rang. "Excusez-moi, I left this as a contact number; it is likely for me."

He lifted the receiver. "Robillard. Oui," listening for a few minutes he then spoke in rapid French and I caught the name Valin. Eventually he finished and returned to us.

"I have organised for Monsieur Valin to be found and brought in for questioning. I have also been informed how the thieves were able to enter your villa undetected."

We all waited with bated breath.

"Both locks on the gates along the private steps to the beach have been forced."

"Oh my word, I never even thought of that."

"I don't think any of us did, Elspeth."

"I have arranged for them to be mended and you will be provided with a new key."

"Captain Robillard, I am concerned these thieves will come back. Are you able to provide any sort of additional security for us?"

"Yes, Miss Bridges, I am. I will arrange for two armed guards for round the clock protection at the villa. These will be men of my own choosing, men I trust and who will report directly to me. I am also pleased to tell you the villa has been cleaned and put back to how it was, you may return home whenever you like."

"There is one other thing," I said, rising and bringing back the newspaper from the breakfast table. "Do you remember the couple I told you about last night? Well, a photograph of them is in the paper this morning." I pointed it out and passed it across.

"They look even more like wraiths in black and white. You described them well. I'll get the original photograph from the newspaper offices and begin to search for them. Thank you."

He put the newspaper down and once more thumbed through his notebook. "There is the name of a couple unaccounted for from the guest list. It could be them but so far a search has brought up nothing. It may of course be a false name…"

Again the telephone bell sounded and he went to answer it. This time although he controlled it well we all saw he was angry. Replacing the receiver none too gently he turned to us, eyes flaming.

"Monsieur Valin has gone missing."

***

It was rather a sober journey back to the villa; I could see mother still felt responsible for Clementine's death even though we had all tried to convince her she wasn't to blame. Pierre had his nose buried deep in the newspaper and my aunt was leaning back against the seat with her eyes closed. I gazed out of the window with unseeing eyes, the confusing elements of the case whirling around my brain like grains of sand caught up in a storm.

Adele and the butler both greeted us at the door when we arrived, both disbelieving at the two shocking events the night before and full of apologies for not being present to prevent the break-in.

"Nonsense," my mother told them. "I gave you both the night off, and in hindsight it was a fortuitous decision. You could both have been hurt."

The villa looked much as it had done upon my arrival with no outward signs it had been riffled through by thieves, although there was an air of violation, particularly hard for my mother, but which we all felt to one degree or another.

We left Adele to unpack our bags. "Where shall I put these, Madame?" she asked of the paintings Pierre had returned.

"Oh just leave them against the wall there. Monsieur DuPont may wish to continue his studies."

The rest of the morning was spent doing nothing much at all, which I found terribly frustrating, so after lunch I announced I was going to walk into the small town if anyone wished to join me. Mother and Pierre both declined but Aunt Margaret said she would.

We once again took the coastal path and I was relieved to see the gates to the beach had been replaced with something much sturdier, and a police guard was already in place. We bid him good afternoon and continued on our way.

"So, Ella, now it is just the two of us, you can tell me your thoughts. I assume you feel as I do that the three events are connected in some way?"

"Of course, it's too much of a coincidence otherwise."

"And the captain is of the same opinion?"

"He said as much last night. The entire burglary is incredibly odd though, if it were just a random act by amateurs who either came upon an empty property or had been watching a few in the hope owners and staff would leave at some point, then they would have taken whatever they could lay their hands on. If they were professionals looking for something in particular, as we have to think they were if we believe the cases are connected, then surely they would have taken something to disguise their true motive? It makes me wonder if they were hired by a third party to search for the specific item, but not given additional instructions, like 'make it appear to be a genuine burglary,' for example, and were too stupid not to think to do that themselves. And I can't think what they were looking for."

"And what of the murder?"

"It was undoubtedly staged."

"In what way?"

I explained what I had told Captain Robillard about the clothes. "And the way she was displayed under the easel at the time when the gallery was to be full just confirms it. I believe it was a message to someone."

"Valin perhaps?"

"That is my train of thought at the moment, I'll admit. He was there at the gallery and left shortly after the unveiling but before the police arrived to question him. He had an argument with Clementine which we were witness to, and we overheard the telephone conversation where he complained quite vociferously about her. Add that to the fact he has now disappeared and there can be no doubt as far as I can see he is involved in some way."

"You don't think he was responsible for her murder but that she was murdered in order to keep him in line perhaps?"

"That's my idea yes, although I could be proved wrong. Regardless, he is involved in whatever is going on otherwise why would he run? I think he is in fear for his life from whomever he spoke to on the telephone and whoever that was, murdered or ordered the murder of Clementine."

"Are the police going to be able to find out who he spoke to?"

"I hope so but it may be difficult, it will all depend on what the operator can remember. But while it was the phone in the art school office, we can only give an approximate time of when it occurred and I expect the line is a busy one. Trying to pinpoint the exact call may prove impossible but Captain Robillard will certainly be pursuing it. Of course all it will take is for the person Valin spoke with to deny they had anything to do with the murder, even if they agree they had spoken to Valin and what the conversation entailed. It would be up to us to prove it, that's the most difficult part. I don't suppose I explained that very well, did I?"

"Oh I see how complicated it all is, and I believe you meant something along the lines of, telling several truths to hide a lie."

"That's it exactly, clever of you."

"I believe Tennyson wrote something similar. Then

to muddy the waters even further we have this young couple undoubtedly complicit in some way, but who've also disappeared. Then there's the poor colonel."

"We need to find the couple urgently. They are our best lead so far as it's obvious they know something. I do hope we find Colonel Summerfield safe and well soon but I can't help thinking he's blundered into something completely by accident which has endangered his life."

"Tell me honestly, Ella, do you think Colonel Summerfield is still alive?"

I sighed. "I don't know, Aunt Margaret. But considering all that has happened so far I'm afraid we need to be prepared for the worst."

※

The small town square was busy when we arrived and quite beautiful with the sun glinting off the pastel-coloured buildings and shop glass. Lovers strolled arm in arm peering in shop windows and pointing at the goods on display, sharing coy smiles and infectious giggles. Nannies pushing perambulators or holding tight to their charges' hands strode in groups, their navy, white and grey attire marking them out as professionals. The eateries were doing a good trade with the pavement tables, under their gaily-coloured umbrellas, full to capacity. I saw housekeepers and maids in smart uniforms scurrying about their business with baskets laden with long French loaves, stopping to place orders in the numerous delicatessens and patisseries. Smells of strong coffee and vanilla drifted on the breeze, joined by the lemon and sugar of the street vendors making crêpes for the crowd, and the whole was overlaid with the fragrant scents of flowers, which were arranged in baskets hanging overhead and planters along the entire length of the street.

We stopped to gaze in windows full of antique furniture, artfully arranged shoes and fashionable clothes. I paused to peruse a stand of postcards while my aunt studied the shelf of old books, and that was when something brushed my ankle. I jumped and looked down and saw Phantom.

"Oh!"

"What is it, Ella?"

"I'm not sure just yet."

I watched Phantom cross the square and immediately my eye was caught by a gentleman opposite; it was the apparition from the aeroplane. I was struck this time by just how familiar he seemed, not because I'd seen him before but because I had seen someone who looked like him recently. A split second later a couple exited the shop behind. The young woman turned to her companion and the strap of her dress moved slightly displaying a rose-coloured birth mark on her shoulder.

"Aunt Margaret, it's them!" I hissed, grabbing her arm and pulling her behind the card stand.

"Who?"

"The couple from the gallery, over there just coming out of the perfumery."

"But it looks nothing like them, they're both dark. I thought you said the couple were pale and blond?"

"Well, it was obviously a disguise this is definitely them, I recognise the birth mark on her shoulder. I completely forgot about it until now but I saw it that night when she turned and gripped the man's arm. Oh gosh, I didn't tell Captain Robillard about it either."

"It can't be helped. What do you suggest?"

"We need to follow them and find out where they go. It could give us clue to their identity but they might recognise us. I could find a telephone and ring the captain but it would take too long. We'll just have to risk it."

I started to move forward but Aunt Margaret grabbed my arm, "Stay there and don't lose them. I'll be back in a minute."

She dashed down the street for a couple of yards and disappeared into a shop. I kept my eye on the couple and watched as they slowly strolled down the street, moving further and further away. I was just about to go after them when my aunt reappeared, arms full.

"Here put this little lot on. Two can play at disguises."

She handed me a long duster coat in light coloured linen, a gay floral scarf to cover my hair and a pair of sunglasses. She was dressed the same except her duster coat was laurel green.

"Right come along, darling, we don't want to lose them. We'll just leave our hats here and pick them up on the way back if they're still here."

"You've done this before," I said, observing our reflections in the windows as we strode by. I was amazed at how different we looked.

"Once or twice," she replied with a smile. "Although this is the first time I've been motor car racing in France."

"I'm sorry?"

"We need a story and I have a plan. Just follow my lead."

"All right, I just hope they don't get into a motor car themselves or we're sunk."

We followed at a discreet distance but never lost sight of our quarries. They were oblivious to our existence thankfully and never once looked round. As we followed them away from the main town up winding back streets and out along a road, which commanded magnificent views of the sea, we dropped back a little and hid behind trees and in hedges. Eventually they turned down a small street and took a right turn. Peering round the corner, we saw their destination was a pair of large wrought iron gates a few yards away.

"It's now or never, Ella," my aunt said, then strode out and turned into someone completely different.

"I say! You there! Hello, can you hear me?"

The couple who realised the loud aristocratic voice behind was aimed at them, turned slowly in surprise.

"Dashed nuisance," my aunt said when she'd reached them. "But the bally motor's conked out, steam everywhere. Gasket probably, 'bout to blow my own as a matter of fact. I say, do you speak English?"

"Yes, Madame," replied the man.

"Splendid! Lady Hamilton-Wyke," she said, thrusting out a hand and pumping his madly. "Just call me Dolores. This here is Partridge, my navigator."

I nodded once but remained silent.

"Now, got a telephone I can use? Need to catch Smithers my mechanic before he leaves. There's a pretty pot in this race and I'll be dashed if I'll lose it to Ponsenby, never hear the end of it."

It was a sublime bit of acting and the couple were taken in hook line and sinker. Seconds later we were through the gates and walking down the drive to a large villa. I walked behind and listened to my aunt as she continued to regale the surprised couple in the joys of European cross country motor racing. By the time we were in the drawing room where the telephone was I believed every word myself.

While my aunt was getting through to 'Smithers,'

I looked at the photographs arranged on the table. One was the face of a man I knew well, the spirit who had been following me since the aeroplane. This was why he looked familiar. The features were an older version of the couple in front of us; there was obviously a family connection. I breathed a sigh of relief as it dawned on me the ghost was not Colonel Summerfield as I had thought it might have been when I first saw him. I tapped it gently, hoping Aunt Margaret would take the hint, then settled down to wait.

"Smithers, that you? Thank god I caught you. The motor's died on me. Yes, steam everywhere. Gasket? Yes, that's what I thought. Need it fixed or we'll miss the next check point. Where am I? Haven't a clue, hang on."

She turned to me then shook her head. "No good asking you, rum navigator you turned out to be."

"Oh do pipe down, Dolly," I said in my most insolent aristocratic drawl. "If you'd turned left when I told you instead of right we'd know exactly where we are."

Her mouth twitched slightly and I knew the eyes beneath the dark glasses were filled with laughter.

"And if I had we'd have been stuck in the middle of nowhere with no telephone at all." She turned to the couple. "Where are we?"

They gave her the name of the villa and the nearest town, which she passed on to Smithers.

"Got that have you? Murder? What murder?"

I saw the shock on the couple's faces immediately.

"A gallery you say? What shooting? Oh art, not my bailiwick, Smithers, you know that. Can't tell a Turner from a Turnip. All right how long? In the town? Yes, all right see you then. And, Smithers, I'll call back if you're not there pronto, understand? Good man."

The couple had visibly relaxed once they'd heard my aunt say she knew nothing about art and by the time she turned there was no trace of their discomfort.

"So, jolly nice place you have here. Is it yours?"

"It belongs to our uncle."

"Is he here? Like to say thanks for the use of the telephone."

"No, I am afraid he is currently out sailing."

"Oh well, can't be helped. Is this him?" she said pointing to the photograph I had tapped.

"Yes," the young man said. So far the girl hadn't said a word.

"Handsome chap," my aunt said. "Reminds me of the Duke of Worcester. Now then, what's all this about a murder? Smithers said someone was shot in an art gallery?"

"She was not shot," the girl said, earning her a swift look from her sibling, for now it was obvious to me they were brother and sister, and not only that but twins.

"Oh Smithers never gets it right. Were you there?"

."No we were not; we have read about it in the newspapers however. Now if there is nothing else...?"

"No, that's it. You have my undying gratitude for the use of the telephone, and do be careful if there is a murderer loose. Honestly I don't know what the world is coming to; it's a good job we're just passing through. Come on then, Partridge, might as well have some tea while we're waiting. Cheerio, we'll see ourselves out," and with a final wave over her shoulder we marched out the door, up the drive and through the open gate.

We continued our charade all the way to town in case we were being followed, but once we were safely seated at the back of a little tea-room where we couldn't be seen or heard, we removed our disguises and returned to normal.

"Aunt Margaret, that was inspired. Quite brilliant in fact."

"You're a natural yourself, Ella. Dolly indeed!"

"So who exactly is Smithers? I know you spoke with someone."

"Pierre. He knows Dolores."

"Oh but I've just had a dreadful thought. What if they ring the operator and ask to be put back through to the previous number? They'll know it was all a sham."

"I expect them to. But Pierre and I have a code; he's sitting by the phone as Smithers now waiting for them. Don't worry, it will be fine, but on the off chance our ruse is detected we know where they live. It will be a simple job for Captain Robillard to find their identity now. However, we don't want them to run before Robillard's had chance to interrogate them, hence my man Smithers."

"I need to call the captain. Can you order tea while I ask to use the telephone here?"

The public telephone box was to the rear of the tea-room and was empty. I entered then closed the door, the light overhead switching on automatically when the door closed. Sitting on a velvet chair I lifted the receiver and asked to be put through. It was only a few seconds later when I heard a strange and surprisingly English voice at the other end.

"Hello, may I speak with Captain Robillard, please? It's Ella Bridges."

"I'm terribly sorry, Miss Bridges, but I'm afraid the Du-ahem, the captain, is not in."

"Oh I see. Sorry who am I speaking to?"

"Beecher, Miss Bridges, I am the butler."

"An English butler?"

"Indeed, Miss."

"Do you know when the captain will return?

"I believe tomorrow. However, he usually telephones in the evening. Can I pass on a message?"

"Oh dear, it's rather important?"

"In that case I do have a way to leave urgent messages for him. Would that suffice?"

"Yes please, could you tell him I know who the couple are, not their names but where they live?"

I proceeded to give him all the necessary details and after he assured me he would contact the captain post haste to leave a message, I thanked him and returned to my aunt.

"Did you speak with him?"

"No, the butler took a message."

"The butler?"

"Yes, the *English* butler."

"My, my."

"Aunt Margaret, how many French police captains do you know who have an English butler? Or any butler for that matter."

"I don't know any other French police captains."

"And who drive very smart, very new and very expensive sports cars and who studied at Oxford?"

"Yes, I see your point."

"And I swear the butler was about to say something else and hurriedly changed it to captain."

"Really?"

I nodded. "I don't think Jacques Robillard is everything he makes himself out to be."

✸

"So you took Dolores out of the cupboard and dusted her off, did you?" Pierre asked my aunt on our return home, his eyes twinkling with merriment.

"I did indeed. Did you get a telephone call?"

"Of course, the operator put them through again almost immediately, but rest assured they are no longer suspicious you are home and dry as the saying goes."

"What was the code you talked about, Aunt?"

"Do you remember me saying to 'Smithers' I would call back if he was not there to meet us?"

I nodded.

"Well that was the code. Pierre would then know another call would be likely, to answer it himself and to keep up the pretense."

"Very clever," I said. "Tell me when did Dolores first make her appearance?"

"Do you know I can't quite remember, dear."

Pierre coughed and was awarded a stern glare from my aunt. He held up his hands in mock defeat. I would get no help from that quarter.

I sighed. "I'll get to know one day I hope?"

"Perhaps I'll write my memoirs, darling. Published posthumously of course."

I laughed. "All right. So where is mother?"

"She is resting," Pierre said. "Quite worn out with everything but she will be fine do not worry."

We heard the telephone bell then and a moment later Adele came in, "Mademoiselle Bridges, it is Capitaine Robillard."

"Good evening, Captain Robillard," I said upon lifting the receiver.

"Miss Bridges, I apologise for being absent when you telephoned. I am currently in Nice."

"Yes, your butler said you were away. Are you on the trail of the colonel?"

"I am making inquiries. However the trail, if there was one, has gone cold."

"But he did definitely arrive in Nice?"

"Yes. I have spoken with two of the railway staff, a porter and a ticket collector, both of whom remember him getting off the train and leaving the station. He turned left on foot and after that I am sorry to say there is nothing."

"Have you... have you checked the hospitals?"

"I have and there is no sign of him in any of them. I also checked the mortuaries and again nothing. To my mind, Miss Bridges, there is only one or two possibilities: either he has been kidnapped or killed and the body disposed of in such a way we will never find it."

"Or both," I said softly.

"I'm afraid that is also possible, I'm sorry. But try not to lose hope. We will keep looking. I also have some news regarding the murder of Madame Dubois. The cause of death was an overdose of heroin, *two* needle puncture wounds were found during the post-mortem examination and there was a significant amount found in her system."

"Oh my word, how dreadful! But you emphasised two needle marks. Is that significant?"

"I think so. I believe the first may have been used to make her more pliable, to allow her to be dressed as she was to get her into the gallery without arousing suspicion and place her where she was found. The second was the overdose that killed her and I believe this to have been done once she was under the easel."

"How on earth could someone do that without being seen?"

"Monsieur Tuel had hired several agency people to help set up for the gala, people he did not know personally. He left much of the work to them and played overseer and he was elsewhere much of the time. According to him the paintings were placed on easels to his satisfaction, after that he simply said to cover them and left them to it. I think it was during this time the body was placed and one or more of the temporary employees was on hand to ensure no one went near. There is, as you would expect, a rear entrance to the gallery where exhibits are delivered and unloaded privately. The agency is being looked into now."

"But why would they dress her as they did?"

"To avoid suspicion if by chance they were seen. She simply would look like a guest coming early to the show."

"Yes, I suppose that makes sense. Is there any news of Monsieur Valin?"

"Nothing as yet but we are watching his home and the school premises. Now tell me of this couple at the gallery. You know where they are I understand?"

"Yes, Aunt Margaret and I were shopping in the town this afternoon and I saw them leave the perfumery. They looked very different with dark hair and he was clean shaven, obviously they had disguised themselves for the gallery visit. I saw the birthmark on her shoulder when she turned at the gallery that evening. I apologise for not telling you sooner but it had completely slipped my mind."

I could hear him scratching notes as I spoke. "No matter, please continue."

"Well, it all started when Aunt Margaret decided to dust off Dolores. She'd come back from a nearby shop with perfect disguises..."

"Disguises?"

"Yes, I wasn't convinced at first but they worked like a charm. So we followed them..."

"Who or what is Dolores?"

"She's a sort of persona of Aunt Margaret's, a character if you like. I've never met her before but apparently she's used her in the past to great effect."

"You talk as though she is real?"

"Well, if you'd been there you'd be hard pushed to believe she wasn't. I was Partridge, her long suffering navigator. It was a splendid performance and the twins were completely taken in."

"The couple are twins?"

"Yes. Aunt Margaret telephoned Pierre who was pretending to be her mechanic Smithers because we were in a motor race and had broken down, and of course when we left they had the operator call back, just to check our credibility I suppose but Pierre had understood the code my aunt used; they'd used it before apparently and continued the ruse."

I heard the tearing of paper over the line followed by a long sigh. "Miss Bridges, perhaps you could start again from the beginning? I am, to use one of your own words, completely baffled."

I started again and went more slowly while Captain Robillard made notes and asked questions to clarify certain points.

"I think I have a much clearer picture now, Miss Bridges. Do you realise how reckless this escapade of yours was?"

I was rather taken aback at his vexed tone.

"There was no harm done, Captain Robillard, and..."

"That is not the point. Following them to their villa is one thing, entering is quite another. Did you stop to think if they were alone? What if the murderer had been present? Would you and your aunt have been able to escape if attacked? No, I do not think so, it was irresponsible and how could I forgive myself if you had come to harm?... either of you?"

He gave an exasperated sigh and I imagined him running his hand through his hair in frustration. His comments had hit me like a hammer. He was perfectly correct. Neither my aunt nor myself had thought any further than getting through the door. If the twins had not been alone then the outcome could have been completely different. And we hadn't even been able to tell anyone where we were going. It was a stupid mistake and one I'm sure I wouldn't have made had I been in England. But his cadence still riled and my own idiocy had made me quite cross, so it was with a quite frosty tone I answered.

"I apologise, Captain. You're quite right, it was foolhardy."

"What is your aunt's history exactly? And how does Pierre DuPont fit in?"

"Honestly? I have no idea. It's all rather hush hush and no matter how many times I ask her she refuses to tell me. As far as Pierre is concerned, they have been friends for a long time."

"I see. Well, I shall arrange to have a man posted at the twins' villa tonight and will go along myself in the morning. Is there anything else you wish to add?"

"Only that it was very obvious they were both lying when they said their uncle was out sailing. Aunt Margaret and I are both of the opinion they know far more than they are saying. The girl also looked quite drawn and on edge."

The captain didn't speak for some time but there was a rhythmic tapping on the line as well as a faint sound of breathing, so I knew the connection hadn't been lost. I surmised he was deep in thought while tapping his pencil against his notepad. Suddenly he said, "Miss Bridges, I should like you to accompany me tomorrow. I shall pick you up at nine o'clock sharp if that will be convenient?"

"Oh. Yes of course. But what if they recognise me from this afternoon?"

"I hope they do. I shall see you in the morning. Oh and one other thing..."

"Yes?"

"Please come as yourself."

Chapter NINE

AS PROMISED, Captain Robillard rang the bell at nine o'clock precisely. He arrived not in his beautiful sports car as I'd hoped but driving a rather mundane black sedan, no doubt a police vehicle. I was a little disappointed, particularly as I had had the foresight to put Partridge's floral headscarf and dark glasses in my bag.

"Bonjour, Miss Bridges," he said, opening the passenger door then moving around the rear of the vehicle to seat himself behind the wheel.

"Good morning, Captain."

We moved smoothly through the villa gates and turned left toward the hotel, our egress the same gate I had first entered on the journey from the airport. It seemed like many weeks ago but had in actual fact only been a few short days. So much had happened in that time and the relatively simple case of one missing man had suddenly become more and more complex. I wondered if we would ever manage to grasp hold of the separate threads and bring them together to form the complete tapestry.

Soon we had left the complex behind and were shifting gears down a steep winding hill to finally smooth out along the coastal road.

"I feel I need to apologise for last evening," the captain began. "Not..."

"There's no need, Captain, you were quite right in what you said..."

"I know."

Well really!

"I was about to say not for what I said but for the way in which I said it. I was taken by surprise at your actions and was quick to anger; most unusual for me, I am not usually so hot-headed. It was the fear of what *could* have happened, I realise that now."

I eyed him thoughtfully; it was quite refreshing to hear a man admit to a mistake through fear. Not many men would have done so.

"Apology accepted, Captain. But what is done is done; there is no point in dwelling on 'what ifs.' Perhaps we could move forward, and should a similar need for subterfuge be required in the future I shall endeavour to let you know beforehand."

Suddenly he laughed, a deep pleasant sound containing sincere humour and I couldn't help but smile.

"I wonder if I shall ever win an argument with you, Miss Bridges?"

"I didn't realise this was an argument," I replied in genuine surprise, to which he laughed even more. It was quite infectious and I found myself laughing with him. It pleased me, one can hardly maintain an argument if you're sharing laughter, even if in a subtle way you are the butt of the joke.

The journey by car was a much shorter one than it had been on foot and as we rounded a corner I saw our destination on a low hillside to our right. We'd approached from a different angle but there was no mistaking the villa I had visited the day before.

Robillard stopped the car beside a tall hedge and a second later a man appeared. A soft exchange in French took place, then the man disappeared and we moved up the road and parked outside the villa gates. It transpired the man was the police guard put in place the night before; he had informed the captain the twins had been in residence all night and were still there. He had seen no one else enter or leave and was of the opinion they were alone.

A security guard appeared from a hidden booth to the side of the gates, and Captain Robillard flashed his credentials, asking to be announced to the occupants.

"I didn't notice the guard yesterday," I said.

"If you were with the twins then he wouldn't have shown himself, there was no need. He can open the gates automatically from inside the booth."

A moment later the gates swung open and we moved forward, pulling up at the front door just as it opened to expose the twins.

"Don't you think it's odd they have no staff?" I whispered.

"Yes I do, Miss Bridges. Very odd indeed."

The initial introduction was held at the door and in French, however Captain Robillard quickly switched to English.

"This is a colleague from London; I would like therefore to conduct our conversation in English. I know you are both fluent. May we come in?"

We had decided in the car an approach which would not put any emphasis on me would allow me to sit back and observe. I felt sure if they didn't realise who I was initially my identity would dawn on them at some point; until then I would listen unobtrusively and make a mental note of any lies I observed. We were taken through to the drawing room where my aunt and I had been the previous day, but rather than it being a lighthearted conversation, this time it was formal. Captain Robillard and I took seats on the settee at one side of a low glass and chrome table, with a huge wall of windows to our left, while the twins shared a chair opposite. He seated while she sat on the arm, poised I thought to bolt at any moment or to avert her eyes to the view if things became uncomfortable.

I had not removed my dark glasses the day before, and now seeing them properly for the first time without the wigs and make-up and in the boy's case sans the Van-Dyke beard he had worn at the gallery, I realised they were younger than I'd thought, perhaps not yet twenty. Even with a more natural pallor and dark hair they were only slightly less ethereal than in their blond personalities, and just as attractive.

The boy appeared to be quite relaxed, his fingertips steepled in front of him, legs crossed at the knee and with a look of polite yet contemptuous humour, nevertheless the jiggling of his foot suggested otherwise. His sister gazed out of the large windows at the view beyond, hands clasped tightly enough to whiten the knuckles and occasionally flicking a frown my way as she tried to work out who I was. I know I looked considerably different at the gallery exhibition to how I looked sitting in front of them now. My hair was loose and to my shoulders, I had on a plain dress and no jewellery, and barely any cosmetics, but it would only be a matter of time before they made the connection. Whether they would realise I was also Partridge the navigator from yesterday remained to be seen.

"Let me start by asking your names?" the captain began.

"I am Louis Castille and this is my sister Marthe."

"Armand Castille is your uncle, correct?"

"Oui. He is our father's brother."

"And you live with him at his villa here?"

"I do. Marthe is here for the summer only. Our parents travel the orient at the moment."

"I understand you work for your uncle, what is it you do?"

Louis uncrossed his legs and leaned forward, elbows on his knees, hands clasped. "What is this all about, Capitaine? And who is your colleague exactly?" His eyes flicked to me uncertainly.

"Answer my question. What type of work do you do for your uncle?"

Louis sighed. "I am a secretary of sorts, his right hand man if you prefer. My uncle, he has many different business interests you understand. They all run smoothly with my help. This is my job."

Captain Robillard nodded and made notes. "And where is Monsieur Castille at this time?"

"Sailing on his yacht."

"You must be very busy at present, no? With him away sailing, the running of the Castille empire is firmly in your hands."

Louis stood suddenly and went to gaze out of the window. It was apparent to all of us he was doing no work at all and he knew it.

"It is easy for me to do my work from here, besides I am spending time with my sister. Now why exactly have you come here, Robillard?"

"We are investigating a murder."

Louis swung round, eyes wide and face draining quickly of colour. "Impossible! Not uncle Armand?"

Marthe, who up until this point had been gazing at the view, turned her head sharply waiting for the answer, barely controlled fear etched upon her face. It was an interesting display and Robillard took advantage.

"Is there a reason why you think it would be?"

"Stop playing games with us, Capitaine," Marthe said in a furious voice. "Are you here to say Uncle Armand is dead? Murdered?"

"You say impossible, Monsieur Castille," Robillard said, ignoring Marthe for the moment. "Why would you think that?"

"Monsieur-le-duc, yes I have heard of you," Louis addressed Robillard to my utter amazement, "Is my uncle dead?"

He made no show of hearing himself addressed as a duke and I wondered at first if I had misunderstood, but it wasn't as though it could be misinterpreted easily and it would certainly explain the butler.

"Not as far as I know. I am investigating the murder of Madame Dubois at the gallery. You were both there, yet disappeared before my men could question you. I would like to ask you about that."

Their relief was almost palpable upon hearing their uncle was not the subject of our inquiry. However, I was the only one who knew Armand Castille was dead. Whether he had been murdered was impossible to say for certain at this point but the entire case so far, including the reactions and behaviour of his niece and nephew, would add credence to the fact he had got himself embroiled in something dangerous. Plus the fact that his spirit had appeared to me meant he had died in suspicious circumstances; whether it was connected to the colonel's disappearance and the murder of Clementine Dubois I could not say, but I thought it more likely than not.

Becoming uncomfortable from having sat still for so long I repositioned myself, and in doing so something must have caught Marthe's eye for she suddenly jumped up and cried out, "You!"

Robillard said nothing but Louis looked at her in shock. "Marthe, what is it?"

She pointed at me. "Her! She came yesterday with the loud old woman to use the telephone. I thought she was familiar."

Louis glared at me. "You are right, Marthe. What is the meaning of this? Who are you?"

"My name is Miss Bridges, and I am a consultant with Scotland Yard in London."

"Then you are a liar!" Marthe hissed. "You were here yesterday to use the telephone; your motor car had broken down yet now you say you are the English police. How dare you deceive us in this way? You were here to spy on us. Why?"

"Nonsense. I was not here to spy on you at all. I came because you were both guests at the gallery when the body of Madame Dubois was found yet you disappeared almost immediately. That in itself was highly suspicious but even more so was the fact that you gave false names and were both disguised. It would have taken a while to find you although I am sure Captain Robillard and his men would have done so eventually. But it was sheer luck I recognised you in town yesterday and rather than allow you to disappear again I had no choice but to follow you."

"You say you recognised us, how?" asked Louis.

"I admit your costumes were excellent, much better than mine in fact, but the result was the same. As to how," I looked at Marthe. "You have a very distinctive birthmark on your left shoulder."

Marthe gasped and her right hand automatically went to her left shoulder. It was a natural reflex and one which certainly would have given the game away if we hadn't already been certain of who they were.

"You were at Galerie Tuel's the same night also?" Louis asked with a frown as though trying to place me.

"I was. Although I looked far more glamorous than I do now. I find it remarkable how different one can look in a change of clothes, or a different hairstyle with clever cosmetics and accessories. I was with my mother and aunt as part of Monsieur DuPont's party. You know, the artist?"

Marthe had slid down to share the single seat once again occupied by her brother a few moments before, now she tightened her grip on his arm and the brief fear on both their faces was obvious. It lasted but a fraction of a moment but I was in no doubt as to what I had seen. I couldn't explain it, however, it seemed they were more afraid I had been a guest at the gallery than they were of the fact I had infiltrated their home in disguise the day before. It was another mystery to set aside and try to solve later, for now we still had questions to be answered.

Robillard turned to a new page in his notebook. "Why did you go to the gallery in disguise?"

Louis shrugged, outward insolence and bravado now restored. "It is fun, a game. We do it quite often, why not? Where is the harm? We have many different costumes for different occasions."

"But why give false names?"

"Is it not obvious? Giving our real names would make the game worthless. And of course we could not use the characters again for they would be known to be us."

"You left within minutes of the body being discovered, why was that? You must have known we would need to take statements from you."

"It did not occur to us. The gallery was very warm and Marthe was feeling faint, in fact she had just a second before asked to go home."

And there was the little clue which proved the lie. I had seen her flinch a second before the body was discovered. Louis no doubt had realised I may have seen something, he obviously was aware of what his sister had inadvertently done and this was his response. It was quick thinking on his behalf and clever but it was too late: I had seen the lie.

I had learned to notice these small changes in behaviour, posture and facial expressions from Aunt Margaret, who used it as a hobby and a source of entertainment at dinner parties. However, during the murder case at Arundel Hall, Albert Montesford, Scotland Yard's commissioner, had asked if it were a teachable skill. It was, and as a result I had written a textbook, The Art of the Lie, which was now used in British police classrooms as a way to tell when a suspect was lying.

Captain Robillard was continuing his questions but we had both realised whatever advantage we had had was now lost to us; they would stick to this story and tell us no more. If we had managed to question Marthe alone I felt sure she would have broken down but there would be no chance of being able to do that now. Louis was not leaving her side and we could not insist.

"Why did you not come forward later when Mademoiselle Castille was feeling better? It was the correct thing to do, was it not? If you had nothing to hide that is," Captain Robillard said, trying a last attempt to goad them into making a mistake. But it did not work.

"Of course we are not hiding anything; I told you we did not think of it. My concern was to get Marthe home before she fainted. The murder was nothing to do with us. We did not know it was a murder even, until the day after when it was in the newspapers. We did not know the woman. We just wanted to come home and this is what we did. Simple. We can tell you no more."

"You didn't see or hear anything strange or out of the ordinary?"

"Nothing." He stood up, leaving a pale nervous Marthe still seated. "Now if that is all I will show you out."

The captain took his time standing, putting away his notebook and pencil and extracting a business card, which he handed to the boy. "If you think of anything you wish to tell me this is my private number. In the meantime an officer will arrive shortly to take down an official statement."

As I rose to leave I said, "I never told you why I was here in France."

Both the twins looked at me warily. "It does not matter," said Louis.

"Oh but I think it does," I replied looking directly at Marthe. "You see a very dear friend has gone missing. It seems he has vanished into thin air, disappeared without a trace and we are beside ourselves with worry."

I could see my words were having an effect on the siblings; perhaps I could chip their armor even if I could not penetrate it completely. "You see my father died quite a few years ago and my mother has been alone ever since, but here in France I believe she has at last found love and companionship again in her friendship with Colonel Summerfield. But now that has all been wrenched away from her because the colonel has gone.

"Whatever has happened I am convinced it is connected with the murder at the gallery and with the subsequent burglary of my mother's villa. I also think you both know something which you are unable to tell us; perhaps it's to do with your uncle? I don't believe he is away sailing, but I do think you are as much afraid of what has happened to him as I am about what has happened to Colonel Summerfield. Perhaps somebody has told you to keep quiet?

"I'm not asking you to divulge any secrets now, but I would ask that you think about what you are doing and why you are doing it; the lives of two men hang in the balance and the quicker we know what we are fighting the quicker we can act. Perhaps even save their lives. There has already been one atrocious murder remember. You have Captain Robillard's card. If you change your minds or need help then please telephone. Let us help you."

Marthe's eyes had been glistening with unshed tears while I had been speaking and now they spilled over onto her cheeks. She quickly dashed them away and jumped up, running from the room. I looked at Louis who was staring after her a look of wretchedness marring his exquisite features.

"I... I'm sorry, I must go after her. Please see yourselves out." And he followed his sister out of the door and into the room beyond.

Robillard and I moved out of the drawing room and left the villa, closing the door behind us. I had certainly got through to Marthe and Louis at some level, but time would tell whether I had done enough for them to share what they knew.

※

"Would you like some lunch? I can take you home to meet Beecher. He rarely gets to converse with those from his home country; it will be a treat for him. And Mrs Beecher is an excellent cook if you need some additional persuasion," Robillard said as we left the Castille villa and were once more on the coast road heading back toward town.

"I don't need persuading. I'd be delighted."

"I am sorry to hear about your father. It was a brave speech you gave them at the end."

"Not brave, but it was perfectly true. I only hope it does some good."

"I am unsure if we have learned anything at all from them, but the absence of Armand Castille is unusual. I will make some inquiries and see if we can locate him, or if not, find out where he was seen last. It may provide us with another direction we can take our investigation."

"They are both certainly very frightened about something and like you I think their uncle is part of it. Do you know him?"

Robillard shook his head. "Not personally but he is one of the richest men in France so of course I know of him. Occasionally we have been at the same social events but I have not spoken more than a word or two with him, and nothing of import."

"What is his business?"

"Anything and everything. To use an English expression, he has his fingers in many pies, from import and export, shipping, arts and antiques even restaurants and the theatre. He owns many properties both commercial and private, here and in the cities; Nice, Paris, Marseille. Wherever there is an opportunity to make money you will find Armand Castille."

I mulled over this information as we continued to drive past the town and up into the hills beyond.

"Are you able to find out more information about his business dealings? I am particularly interested in the arts and antiques you mentioned. It may be nothing but Colonel Summerfield, Madame Dubois and Monsieur Castille all have art as a connection, somewhat tenuously in the case of the colonel but we shouldn't dismiss it. I also wonder if this area of Armand Castille's business is dealt with in part by Louis Castille?"

"There may be something in what you say, Miss Bridges! It is good reasoning. I shall make some telephone calls from my home. We are almost there."

Home for Captain Jacques Robillard was a large, historic and beautifully appointed villa with formal gardens, a fountain and a hedge maze. The interior was a clever mix of modern juxtaposed with old pieces from centuries before handed down through the generations.

Beecher had been delighted to see a fellow Britisher and we talked of life in England while Robillard used the telephone. When he returned Beecher escorted us through the drawing room and out to a seating area with tented ceiling, and commanding views of the formal garden and the sparkling water beyond.

"Luncheon will be served shortly, Sir, Mademoiselle."

"Thank you, Beecher. Miss Bridges, what would you like

to drink? Wine, exceptionally good homemade lemonade or perhaps one of Beecher's, exquisite cocktails?"

"Oh, I'll try a cocktail please."

"Make that two, Beecher."

"Yes, sir."

"You have a very beautiful home, Captain Robillard."

"Thank you. It has been in my family for many generations, and please call me Jacques. I feel we have moved on from such formality, don't you?"

I nodded. "Yes I think we have, it's Ella. So you are a duke?"

"I wondered if you had caught that. Yes, my official title is Duke of Angoulême, it's a duchy in the West. It has a long history but now we are famous for our sunflowers and our Cognac."

"Being a police captain seems very far removed from being a duke. How do you balance the two when you have a duchy to run?"

He laughed. "It is a very small duchy and means much less than it used to in the past. Now I am more what you would call a gentleman farmer and a mostly absentee one. I leave the vast majority of affairs to my estate manager and the staff."

Beecher arrived then with the cocktails. "I thought the Soixante Quinze, most apt for today, sir."

"The Seventy Five, yes a good choice."

I took the tall champagne flute and sipped carefully.

"That's quite perfect, Beecher," I said. "What's in it?"

"Champagne, Gin, although Cognac may be used as an alternative, sugar, lemon juice and a secret ingredient of my own, Miss Bridges."

I laughed. "Of course it would contain a secret ingredient. Well, it's quite delicious."

He smiled, gave a small bow and removed himself to see to the luncheon.

"Why did you choose to become a policeman?" Jacques was quiet for a minute and I wondered if I had been too intrusive. "I apologise. I'm asking too many questions."

"No, no, not at all. I told you my mother died when I was young? Well, it was through violence; she was in the wrong place at the wrong time and was shot. She died immediately but the perpetrator was never caught. In fact he remains free to this day, assuming he is still alive; it was nearly twenty five years ago."

"Jacques, I am most terribly sorry."

"It was a long time ago, Ella, but it gave me a respect for the law and a desire to uphold it. Ah, here is our lunch. Bon appétit."

※

After a wonderful lunch Jacques drove me back to my mother's where I found everyone resting in the garden.

"Hello, darling, how did you get on?"

I told them all about the interview with the twins and their obvious fear of something or someone, which was preventing them from speaking candidly, as well as the fact their uncle had vanished.

"Do you think the cases are connected, Ella?" my aunt asked.

"Yes I do, and what's more so does Jacques. He's looking into the Castille businesses and will let me know if he finds anything."

"You are on a first name basis now? About time too," my mother said with a quick knowing glance at my aunt, which I pretended not to see.

"It means nothing, it's just so much easier than referring to titles all the time, like captain or duke, don't you think?"

"Duke?" they both said together. "Captain Robillard is a duke? A real one?" mother asked.

"Yes, he holds a small duchy in the west apparently."

"How interesting," said my aunt in musing tones. "We may have known his father, or perhaps his grandfather, what do you think, Pierre?"

"It is possible." He replied from behind his newspaper.

We were then interrupted by Adele who informed me there was a telephone call. "Monsieur Baxter, Mademoiselle."

I dashed inside and picked up the receiver. "Hello, Baxter."

"Hello, Miss Bridges. How are things in France?"

I quickly brought him up to date.

"Good grief! A murder, a robbery and another missing person? Sounds as though you've disturbed a hornet's nest there and no mistake. Well, I'm afraid I'm about to add to your troubles. Turns out Colonel Summerfield is one of ours."

"Baxter! Do you mean he is a detective?"

"Undercover."

"Oh my word, this changes everything. I take it he isn't retired but on an active case?"

"As far as I know, but I'm running up against a lot of closed doors here and I'm afraid they won't tell me anything. Different department and all that, it's international crime and I don't have the necessary clearance."

"So you don't even know why he is here?"

"No clue at all I'm afraid. I'm waiting for the commissioner to get back to me, see if he can call in some favours higher up; I've already called in more than I had to get this far."

"Is Summerfield his real name?"

"No, but I don't know what it is so no point in asking. The Colonel Summerfield retired British army chap I was looking into doesn't exist once you get passed the surface stuff."

"Baxter, do you think he is he working for Interpol?"

"That would be my guess. Headquarters are in your neck of the woods aren't they? Lyon, I believe."

"Baxter, that's miles away."

"About three hundred or thereabouts. You're still nearer than me though," he said with a chuckle.

"Oh it's practically impossible for me to do anything at this end, and who's to say if I did manage to get there whether they will talk to me? I doubt a telephone call will be much use, especially from an Englishwoman with no jurisdiction and who can't speak the language. I don't have clearance either. The only thing I can do is to pass what you've told me on to Captain Robillard and see if he can pursue matters. Gosh, Baxter, this really has taken the wind out of my sails. I didn't expect this news at all."

"You and me both. Well I'll continue to push at the bureaucratic nonsense at this end, although it could take days. I'll telephone whenever I have information."

"I wonder if they know one of their men is missing?"

"Don't you doubt it for a minute, Miss Bridges; they'll know all right and will be pursuing their own inquiries. Whether they let us in on what they know is another matter."

"I hope they do, Baxter, for his sake because I am failing miserably."

I walked back into the garden where Aunt Margaret and Pierre were eagerly awaiting news.

"Ella, you look dreadful, what did Baxter say?"

"Where's mother?"

"Just gone in to get her book. Why, what's happened?"

"It's Edward Summerfield. He's not a retired army colonel at all. He's an undercover detective working on a case, probably for Interpol. Summerfield isn't even his real name but Baxter doesn't know what is. How on earth am I going to tell mother?"

"There's no need to tell me, Ella. I heard every word."

Chapter TEN

I TURNED AND SAW MY MOTHER walking towards us, book in hand and her face pale and drawn. I met her halfway across the patio and enveloped her in a hug.

"I'm so sorry, mother," I whispered.

Her grip tightened for a moment, then relaxed and she drew back. "It's all right, Ella, and really it's hardly your fault. But are you quite sure?"

I nodded.

"Well it seems I've been lied to and been made to look a complete fool."

"That's only one way to look at it you know and honestly I'm not sure it's the right one," I said softly.

"And just how would you interpret it? The man I knew as Edward Summerfield doesn't exist; he's a complete stranger."

I remembered thinking something similar a few weeks prior. My husband John was dead. In fact he'd died twice, and he was not who I had thought him to be either. It had been a huge wrench and an emotional roller-coaster the likes of which I had never experienced before, nor ever wished to again. The news had come in the middle of a particularly trying case and I had nearly missed valuable clues while my mind had been distracted.

"I know something of what you are feeling, mother."

"Oh darling, of course you do! I'm sorry, I wasn't thinking. I just feel like such a fool to have been taken in like this. I honestly thought I was a better judge of character."

"It's a perfectly natural response and I daresay the anger will follow. But I truly believe this was not intentional on Edward's behalf. From what you've told me of him I think he really has fallen for you and tried his utmost to protect you while still doing the job he came here to do."

"Do you really think so, dear? I hope you're right. But it doesn't really matter who he is, does it? I still care for the man I know and I'm more worried than ever about him now."

"It changes the whole aspect of the case knowing he is working officially on something which requires him to be undercover, and he's obviously closed in on something. Unfortunately, until we hear from Baxter we have no idea what it is. I need to telephone Jacques and let him know."

"You go ahead, dear. I think we'll all move indoors; we should discuss what we know so far. I'll ask Adele to bring drinks shortly."

I telephoned Jacques on his private number but Beecher informed me he was out. I left a message for him to telephone me at mother's villa as soon as he could as I had important news and then went to join the others in the drawing room. Mother was correct. If we discussed everything we knew to date, perhaps we could shed some light on the entire mystery, which in turn would lead us to the man we knew as Edward Summerfield. It was apparent now his life was in imminent danger.

"So what do we actually know so far, Ella?" Aunt Margaret asked as the four of us settled in the drawing room. We began to discuss the happenings to date, but I could see Pierre was becoming impatient. Suddenly he jumped out of his chair and began to pace in front of the open French windows.

"But there must be something to link all of these happenings, no?"

"It's art in one way or another," I said.

"Precisement! It is art!" said Pierre excitedly. "Let us go through it again with this in mind. Firstly the colonel disappears. He is a student of the art school. Then Madame Dubois is murdered at a gallery and she runs the art school. Next this villa is broken into; why we do not know at this moment but there will be a connection I am sure of it. Next Monsieur Valin who teaches at the art school disappears. The millionaire Castille, poof! He is also gone and is known to have business connected with art. His niece and nephew who were at the gallery know of something to make them afraid. The colonel is then discovered to be an English policeman working undercover. And then there is this!"

Pierre snatched a newspaper from the table and opening it showed us a small news item on page six. "Eh voila!"

"What does it say?" I asked.

Mother shook the paper, read it quickly, then proceeded to translate it briefly for us. "It is a continuation of previously reported news I think."

"Indeed!" agreed Pierre. "I have been following this news since we arrived, every day another little bit of information."

"But what is it *about*, Pierre?" Aunt Margaret asked impatiently.

"There have been a number of thefts of paintings," my mother read aloud. "From private residences all across France. Oh my goodness, it says they are some of the most valuable and well known works of art in the world, all by the great masters. All in private collections and all have disappeared without a trace."

We looked at Pierre. "And you think this is connected with what is happening here?" Aunt Margaret asked him in grave tones.

I wondered for an instant if this was a stretch too far, but it seemed to fit all the clues of the case. Priceless works of art were being stolen perhaps this was the case Edward was working on? But how did the art school fit in? In the scheme of things it was a very small enterprise. I needed more time to work it all out properly.

"Mais oui! It is art, is it not?"

"Well yes of course it is but it's in an entirely different league altogether, are you suggesting there is a link?"

"Ah, Maggie, Maggie," said Pierre shaking his head and resuming his seat, "I cannot explain how as yet, but yes, I feel it is so."

"I think Pierre is right." I said. "And what's more I feel almost sure this is the case Edward is investigating. We all agree that Edward is most likely a missing Interpol agent, if he has discovered the identity of the gang stealing priceless art then he is in serious danger."

We all heard the telephone bell then and Adele announced it was Jacques returning my call.

"Ella, you have important news I believe?"

"I do, Jacques, and it shines a whole new light on our

investigation. I have heard back from my colleague Baxter at Scotland Yard. Colonel Summerfield is a detective working undercover. He's here on a case."

"Merde!" Jacques exclaimed. "Forgive me, Ella, your news caught me by surprise. As you say this changes everything, I assume your colleague believes the colonel is working for Interpol?"

"We thought probably so, yes. But Summerfield is not his real name. Baxter is still trying to break through the bureaucracy in London to find out who he really is."

"And you don't know why he is here?"

"Not definitely, I'm afraid officialdom has also thwarted any attempt of Baxter's to find out. International crime is above his, actually both of our, positions."

"Mine also, but I need to follow up immediately. As a captain I can only do so much but as a duke perhaps I can do more. I intend to travel to Lyon to see if I can obtain some answers. I shall naturally keep you informed."

"When will you go?"

"Now, there is no time to lose. If a British Interpol agent is here then it's undoubtedly a serious case."

"Yes we came to that same conclusion ourselves."

I told him about the stolen artworks and how we now felt it was this that Edward was investigating.

"Well, the fact he has gone missing raises it to urgent. I need to inform Interpol of our findings and have faith that the information will enable them to find their man. I only hope they will grant me an audience and quickly. The protocol here is just as convoluted as it is in London. I shall telephone when I have news. Adieu, Ella."

"Au revoir, Jacques."

I returned to the drawing room and brought them up to date.

"Ella, do you remember when we first met?" Pierre asked.

"Of course; at your gallery when I was staying with Aunt Margaret."

"And do you remember me telling you about a certain audacious theft I had heard rumours about?"

"A theft from The Louvre, of course, but did we not decide it was impossible?"

He shrugged. "Of course. It is not possible, but after you had solved your case of the clergyman and you had left, these rumours persisted. I believe there is something in them, not at The Louvre perhaps, but elsewhere."

"Didn't you say the grapevine was utterly silent?" I said.

"Indeed, but every single contact I asked knew of no one who was involved, yet the whispers lingered and gained in strength. That in itself is highly unusual."

"Go on, Pierre," my Aunt said, a serious note to her voice.

"The rumours stated it was a British gang of thieves targeting art in France."

"But we don't know the thieves are British, Pierre," my mother said.

"No, but Edward is British, mother," I said. "Why would he be here otherwise if Britain wasn't involved? Perhaps it's a destination for the missing paintings. There are criminal masterminds all over the world. Is it not likely two of them have joined forces to fund such an operation?"

"One English and one French you mean, Ella?"

"Yes."

"Good heavens!" my mother exclaimed. "Have we really stumbled upon something as incredible as international art theft? Surely not? Really it doesn't seem possible, does it?"

But it did to me. The more I thought about it the more convinced I became that this was the real investigation and once again we were right in the middle of it.

※

"Well I don't know about you all but I could do with a stiff drink," mother said. "It's all quite impossible to take in."

"I'll second that, Elspeth. Ah perfect timing, here's Adele now."

Adele entered the room with a loaded tray, then all of a sudden there was an almighty crash and the sound of breaking glass. She'd tripped over the paintings from the art school, which had been left propped against the wall.

"Oh, Madame! I'm so sorry," Adele said and promptly burst into tears as she knelt on the floor to try and clean up the mess.

"Adele, are you hurt?"

"No, Madame," she sniffed. "I tripped on the paintings, I'm sorry, Madame."

"No matter, Adele, it was an accident. Now do stop crying, there's nothing which can't be replaced."

"Are they damaged?" she asked wide-eyed, looking at Pierre who was crouched over the canvasses.

"I doubt it, and it doesn't matter, they were only our amateur efforts. Now go and get a dustpan and brush. You really shouldn't pick up glass with your hands."

While my mother ministered to the hysterical Adele, and my aunt went in search of the butler to assist in the cleaning, I was watching Pierre. Something was wrong. Suddenly he stood up, took my arm and steered me out of hearing of the others.

"Ella, take the paintings to the library at once and wait for us there," he whispered.

"What is it, Pierre? You've found something I know you have!"

"The most important clue of all!" he said, eyes shining in excitement.

"Very enigmatic, Pierre. But now is not the time to be cryptic. Tell me what you've found."

"You sound just like Maggie," he chuckled. "Now go, we cannot speak in front of the staff. I shall explain soon. I need to collect my bag from the motor car."

I sighed in exasperation, "Fine, I'll find out myself.

Nobody was taking any notice as I took charge of the canvases and whisked them into the library. Closing the door I laid two of them against the bookshelf and studied the one Pierre had been examining. It took me hardly any time at all to make the same discovery. It was astounding and I could have kicked myself for not seeing it sooner. Here was the key to the whole case! And I was left feeling breathless as the threads finally were being pulled neatly into place.

I quickly stacked the paintings facing a bookshelf and hidden by an armchair. No doubt the drinks would be replenished shortly and Pierre had been adamant the staff were to be kept ignorant of his findings. Now I knew why. I paced up and down in a state of nervous excitement waiting for the others.

Pierre, Aunt Margaret and my mother entered a moment later followed by the butler with a new tray and a still tearful Adele, carrying a tantalus as though it were a newborn, so determined was she not to repeat her previous clumsiness. Once they had left and the door closed, my aunt asked the all-important question.

"Is that Irish or Scotch Whiskey, Elspeth?"

"I have no idea. Here, try it and see."

"Thank you, my dear. Now, Pierre, would you mind telling us why we've all been summoned to the library? I feel as though I'm in a mystery novel and you're about to accuse one of us of murder."

"Pah! Nothing so cliché, Maggie. No, I have through my supreme intelligence and prowess solved the mystery!"

"Good lord, Pierre, I rather think you need to look up the meaning of the word cliché."

Pierre ignored my aunt's teasing and turned to me. "Ella, the paintings if you please. Put them on this table here."

I did as he asked; laying the canvases side by side so they could be viewed properly, and waited impatiently for the penny to drop.

"Now what do you see, my friends?"

"Oh dear," my mother said. "Adele did do some damage. The corner of Edward's painting here has torn away. It must have been one of the glasses."

"But thanks to Adele's clumsiness I can now see what this whole case is about." I said.

"You can, dear?"

"Look what is underneath the top canvas which Edward painted on!"

Mother and my aunt crowded closer… "Oh, there's

another one, it looks much older," my mother said. "Is that a signature?"

"Where?" my aunt asked, peering closer. She hurriedly put on her spectacles and leaned so close her nose was almost touching the paint. "Good god, it's a Bruegel!"

Chapter ELEVEN

SHE STOOD UP, removed her spectacles and gave Pierre a serious look. He met the stare with an equally serious one. Something non-verbal passed between them as all jokes were set aside and the air became charged with something I couldn't identify.

"I am the first to admit my historical knowledge of the old masters is lacking, but even I can see we have discovered something of vast significance here." I said. "Just how important is this work, Pierre?"

"It could not be *more* important, Ella. Bruegel was the most significant artist of the Dutch renaissance. This painting is over three hundred years old."

"What is it worth?"

"It is priceless."

"Oh my word," my mother said, making her way to a

chair. "How on earth has this happened?"

"It's obvious now that the blank canvases at the art school are very cleverly covering up stolen masterpieces. We need to find out who is behind it." I said.

Aunt Margaret turned from the sideboard where she had poured a finger of brandy for my mother. "I assume this one has been reported as stolen?"

Pierre nodded. "Yes, there was a pair reported stolen several months ago from a chateau not far from Lyon."

"A pair?"

"You have been looking into stolen artwork since we arrived, Pierre?" I asked.

"Oui. Not in relation to our mystery of the colonel but because of what I had heard at home."

"Priceless!" my mother repeated breathlessly. "It's just incredible. Thank heavens it wasn't here when the burglary happened."

We all started as the import of her statement dawned.

"Mother! Of course, this must have been what they were looking for."

"But who would know it was here? Edward gave it to me as a gift. No one but Clementine knew about it. Oh my word that's it isn't it? That's why she was killed?"

"We're not sure of anything at this point, mother, remember. Monsieur Valin was furious with her and complained to somebody about her interference although who we don't know. All the telephone calls for the period have been accounted for and the people spoken to, but no one so far admits to speaking with Valin about Clementine. One thing is certain, however. The art school is at the heart of it all."

"What I would like to know," my aunt said, "is what, if anything, is beneath the other two paintings?"

There was silence while we all glanced at the objects on the table. Pierre went to lock the library door while my aunt drew the curtains and switched on the overhead light. We watched as Pierre open his Gladstone bag and withdrew a canvas wrap. Undoing the ties he rolled it out to reveal several pockets all with various tools of the trade tucked inside. Choosing several, he laid them on the table near to hand and, turning over one of mother's paintings, he gently began to work.

It was a painstaking and meticulous process, but with the possibility of a priceless artwork underneath he was taking no chances. After half an hour, and with only four of the tacks removed, the tension was unbearable so mother went to arrange a cold buffet supper to be brought to the dining room, then gave the staff the rest of the evening off, although they would remain on the premises. Gaston, Pierre's driver, stayed with them and mother informed us that when she had left they were playing cards.

Back in the library with our supper on trays on our knees, we talked quietly while Pierre continued.

"I need to let Jacques know what has happened but he is currently en route to Lyon. I'll have to leave a message with Beecher and hope he telephones for messages soon."

"We can't leave these precious artworks here, Ella; I'll not be able to sleep knowing they are on the premises."

"Don't worry, Elspeth, I'm sure Pierre already has a plan in mind," Aunt Margaret said. "Ella, how do you suppose these paintings came to be underneath the art school canvases? I mean who covered them over?"

"I don't know, Aunt. There was something... no, it's no good, I can't remember. Such a lot has happened recently."

It was quite infuriating knowing there was something I had heard or seen since I had come to France which was important, but try as I might I couldn't bring the memory to mind. I glanced at Pierre who was still concentrating hard on one of the smaller canvasses.

"Excuse me a moment, I'll telephone and leave a message for Jacques."

I closed the library door behind me and rushed to the telephone, making sure the staff were still below stairs. I didn't want the conversation to be overheard.

"Good evening, Beecher."

"Good evening, Miss Bridges."

"I realise the captain is not there at present but I have a message and wondered if you could relay it when he next telephones?"

"Of course, but I assume it is regarding the dinner invitation in two days' time?"

What on earth did he mean? I had received no such invitation, "Well actually..."

"I realise of course you will be accepting but as a matter of formality I will require you to send by return the RSVP *note*."

For a brief moment I wondered if Beecher had been on the sherry while his master was away, then repudiated the idea immediately; it was so completely out of character. I decided to play along and see where it led.

"It will be no trouble to do that, Beecher," I said warily.

"Splendid. Now are you by any remote chance related to the author Jerry Bridges?"

"Yes, he's my brother."

"Wonderful, I am a huge fan of his work. My favourite is 'Notes of Deception,' have you read it?"

I had read all of Jerry's books but Beecher had the title of this one incorrect; it was actually called 'Diary of Deception.' Beecher was obviously trying to tell me something without saying it out loud... suddenly I realised what he meant!

"I understand completely, Beecher, actually it's my favourite too, a very clever story, I particularly like the character of the chauffeur."

"Oh indeed, Miss Bridges, such a useful plot device.

Now is there anything else I can do for you?"

"That's all thank you, Beecher. I'll get the RSVP off to you as soon as I can, and I'm looking forward to the dinner. I'll have Jerry send you signed copies of all his books when I return home."

I replaced the telephone receiver and rushed back to the library. "Mother, do you have writing paper and an envelope handy?"

"Yes, in my room. Oh wait, there's probably some in the study! I never use it which is why I'd forgotten about it. It's an odd little place, completely surrounded by other rooms so there's actually no window." She approached a bookshelf to the left of the library fireplace, removed a book from the third shelf down, just below eye level, then depressed a knot in the wood. With an audible click the whole shelf swung forward on hinges, a remarkably well-concealed door. "Clever isn't it?" she said. "It was the one place the burglars didn't look, too cleverly camouflaged, I expect."

"Gosh, I wonder what it was used for originally," I said as I turned on the overhead chandelier and peered inside a cosy, but beautifully appointed study with a chintz-covered suite in creams and blues and a small writing desk. Pierre, sorry to interrupt but can I borrow Gaston to deliver a message?"

"Oui," he replied without looking up from his work.

I went through to the small study and obtained notepaper from the drawer in the desk. Quickly scribbling a note regarding the finding of the stolen artwork beneath the paintings my mother and Edward Summerfield had done, I placed it in an envelope and addressed it to Jacques. Then asked Gaston to deliver it to Jacques' villa, "Beecher, will also give you a reply if you could wait."

"Certainly, Mademoiselle."

"What was that all about?" Aunt Margaret asked when I returned to the library.

"Beecher being ingenious. Would you believe he talked in code? It took me a while to understand, but once I did I realised he wanted us to communicate via notes, rather than speak over the telephone. I'm sure he thinks someone is listening in."

"It's hardly surprising, considering the money involved in this artifice."

"Eh voila!" Pierre suddenly exclaimed and we all crowded round the table to see what he had uncovered. Gently he lifted the wooden frame, leaving mother's canvas upside down on the table, and turned it over.

The hush was absolute as we stared reverently at the masterpiece laid before us. Even though my knowledge of art was severely limited I knew enough to know this was something extraordinary. It was a small Madonna and child and leaning forward I could make out the signature: Raphael. I glanced at Pierre and noticed as he removed his pince-nez, eyes sparkling with unshed tears. He took a blue silk square from his pocket and wiped his eyes. Actually I rather felt like crying myself, this case was becoming too much too fast; I was now completely out of my depth.

"We are in the company of a true master, my friends. Never in my life did I think this moment would come."

"Do you think the other is also one of his?" my aunt asked, nodding at my mother's second painting as yet untouched.

Pierre nodded. "I would be surprised if not. Raphael painted many Madonna's and I know of two smaller ones the same size as these, which have been stolen. This is one."

"It's painted on a wooden panel, not canvas?"

"Yes, it's been very cleverly concealed; if I had not been suspicious I would not have known. It has also been done by someone with great knowledge, for not only has the original not been damaged in any way but it has been protected, like the Bruegel."

"How old is it?" I asked.

"Over four hundred and thirty years."

"Oh good heavens!" my mother said faintly. "We must telephone the police at once and have them moved to somewhere safe. The thieves may not have found the secret study this time, but who is to say they won't return, despite the guard the captain has in place? I simply won't be able to sleep if they are anywhere on the premises."

Before any of us could explain why that wouldn't be possible there was a knock at the door. I unlocked it to find Gaston holding an envelope. "From Monsieur Beecher, mademoiselle."

"Thank you, Gaston."

"Will there be a reply?"

"I'm not sure yet but if there is I will come and find you."

"Very good, Mademoiselle."

I hurriedly ripped open the envelope and quickly read what Beecher had written, and in doing so I suddenly remembered the important piece of information which had thus far eluded me.

❋

"What does it say, Ella?" Aunt Margaret asked.

"He thanks me for working out his code… and yes, it's as we thought, he believes the telephone conversations are being listened into. He's also told Jacques the same thing."

"Well we will need to be very careful from now on. Carry on, Ella."

"Apparently, Jacques has given him instructions to pass to me any relevant information about the case, and he received some this evening."

"What was it?" mother asked.

"A constable visited the Castille art and antiques business in Nice yesterday, and was given a tour by the manager Monsieur Tremblay."

"Did he find anything suspicious?"

I sighed, "No. According to him everything appeared to be above board."

"Well, he would say that wouldn't he, he doesn't know what he's looking for." My aunt said. "What else does it say?"

"According to this, the business is quite diverse; it exports French antiques, provides art materials to schools…" I looked up at my small audience.

"Art materials including canvases I have no doubt…" I glanced back down at the note, "and the wider community through art shops, the premises of which are owned by the company…" I scanned the letter again trying to pick out the more pertinent parts.

"Louis Castille has been given the work of expanding and developing new business… ah, Castille owns a factory, various warehouses and storage facilities in Nice and other cities across the country, but the Nice premises are the headquarters. We need to go there."

I handed the letter to my aunt and poured myself a drink while she read it and passed it on to the others.

"Do you remember when we were visiting the art school," I said, "Clementine mentioned part of Valin's job was the purchasing and storing of the canvases, but she also said some were donated? What if the donations came from

Castille's business with the masters already hidden beneath?"

"It would explain why he was so angry when we entered the store-room," my aunt said.

I nodded. "And it would explain the telephone conversation we overheard."

"And it would explain how Edward and I have unknowingly painted on top of priceless works of art. Oh good heavens, I'm having palpitations just thinking about it."

"I suspect they are being stolen to order," said Pierre. "Delivered to this factory and disguised, then delivered to the art school. Valin takes control and once they have been used by an amateur in a lesson they are somehow smuggled out of the country."

"Oh!" my mother said. "They must be using the postal service. Don't you remember when we spoke with the others they said some of their work had gone missing?"

"Of course. Well done, mother. This means the paintings are being diverted en route once they have left the country. It's quite a brilliant plan, don't you think? I mean who would suspect anything was untoward regarding a painting done by an amateur holiday maker, who then posted it home?"

"But this means the organisation is far bigger than we anticipated," my aunt said. "And much more dangerous."

Pierre nodded. "Yes, Maggie, you are correct. This is a large scale operation; international organised crime with millions of pounds at stake."

"Whoever is behind this will be searching for these three masters as we speak," I said.

"Oh, I wish I had never got involved with the art school," my mother said. "It was just supposed to be a nice little hobby and I was so enjoying it."

"Mother, were you already enrolled in the classes before you met Edward or was it his idea for you both to join?"

"Oh, I had been enrolled for a long time before I knew Edward. Of course I realise now he probably instigated the idea that he attend with me in order to form a relationship to help with his cover. How utterly maddening!"

"Now, Elspeth, you know that is probably not true. Both Ella and I are convinced his relationship with you, although unexpected, was perfectly genuine. But tell me, had you already painted the gifts for us before then?"

"Oh yes, they took months. I was working on something else entirely by the time Edward turned up. For Jerry and Ginny in actual fact, but it's still in the sketching stage I haven't begun to paint yet."

"And what would you have done with them?"

"Well, if you hadn't been here I would have arranged for them to be posted to you."

"And they would have gone missing," I said. "We would all have naturally been disappointed but would think no more about it."

"Yes. I see what you are hinting at, Ella, that I was

already unwittingly involved before I even met Edward. Why do you suppose he gave me his painting as a gift?"

"For safe keeping," I answered. "I believe he knew what was happening at that point and the only proof he had was the canvas he gave you. But he was taken before he could pursue matters. I doubt very much he thought he would be putting you in danger by doing so, but whoever has him will want to know where the Bruegel is."

"Considering my villa was burgled I suspect they already know."

"But they did not find anything!" said Pierre. "I am hopeful that at present they don't know where it is. But of course they may know about the Raphael's. They are beneath your own work after all."

"We don't know whether Clementine said anything before she died though. If she was unaware of what was happening — and as her friend I truly believe she was completely ignorant of the thefts — then perhaps she didn't tell them anything."

"That may be so, mother. But now we need to step up this investigation for it is becoming more dangerous as each hour passes."

Pierre and Aunt Margaret shared a knowing look.

"What are you both thinking?" I asked, although I could make an educated guess. My thoughts were running in the same direction.

"We need to visit the Castille headquarters in Nice and

take the tour," my aunt said. "It is obviously a large concern with numerous buildings. Plenty of places to hide someone."

"You mean they could be holding Edward there?"

"It's more than possible, Elspeth. We need to find out one way or another, that's certain."

It was decided the two people to go would be Pierre and myself. Should Louis Castille be at the site then he would undoubtedly recognise my aunt and me from previous meetings, particularly if we were together. But if I was to go as an assistant or companion to the world renowned artist Pierre DuPont, who was looking into potential suppliers for his business in England, then we may just get away with it. The obvious fly in the ointment was he had already met me with Jacques.

Aunt Margaret grinned and turned to Pierre. "I do believe it's time to dust off our dressing up box."

I sighed in resignation. It appeared I was going in disguise. Again!

The next morning after breakfast Pierre and my aunt left for Nice. They had informed us the previous evening they would be unable to find what was needed in the small town, but the city had two exemplary costumiers and a perruquier whom Pierre had used before. I had no idea what they were likely to return with. I had learned when the two of them got together almost anything could happen. Their first option had been for me to disguise myself as an elderly spinster, which I had said no to immediately as I couldn't see me being convincing enough. A British reporter commissioned to write an in depth piece about Pierre the artist, also found me shaking my head for the same reason. And I had vetoed in no uncertain terms their plan for me to disguise myself as a male. I just hoped whatever they returned with was something both sensible and plausible.

I had asked them to send a telegram to Baxter from the hotel, explaining briefly our telephone conversations were most probably being listened to, and not to worry about pursuing more about the colonel's activities for we had now found out what he was investigating.

Pierre had locked the paintings in the study the previous evening, much to my mother's dismay, and with nothing more for us to do until he and Aunt Margaret returned, I suggested we tried to forget our worries and force ourselves to relax by having a day at the beach.

"Who do you think is behind all this, Ella?" mother asked, shifting on the sun lounger to face me. "As Pierre said, it must be someone who is familiar with the art world and who has a large organisation at his fingertips. What do you think of this Armand Castille person? Could it be him, do you think?"

I had been wrestling with this very question for a while,

but I knew Armand Castille was already dead and had been since before I had even landed in France. But had he been murdered because he was innocent and had found something out which meant he had to be eliminated? Or was he the mastermind behind the whole affair but had balked at the idea of kidnapping an Interpol agent, therefore signing his own death warrant? Perhaps he was simply the victim of a greedy underling? Whatever the reason, he had been killed in violent circumstances or he wouldn't have shown himself to me on the aeroplane.

"I honestly don't know, mother. He, or his business at least, certainly seems to fit the profile of what we are looking for, but whether he is directly involved remains to be seen. Louis Castille I'm almost sure is involved but not as the mastermind, he's just not clever enough. Besides he is frightened of something."

"And what of Edward? Do you think he is still alive?"

I leaned across and took her hand. "Darling, I honestly don't know but we shouldn't lose hope. Jacques knows there's more to his disappearance than originally reported and I'm sure by now he will have informed Interpol. We will all be doing our level best to find him."

She gave me a wan smile and sat up. "Yes I'll try not to lose hope as you say. I'm going for a swim. I think the exercise will help me take my mind off things. Perhaps it will help me sleep better too."

I lay on my lounger and watched her walk across the sand toward the blue water, praying our hope of the man we knew as Edward Summerfield still being alive wasn't misplaced.

※

Aunt Margaret and Pierre returned just after six o'clock that evening laden with bags and parcels, followed by the butler, Adele and Gaston, all equally weighed down. Once the staff had left we moved everything through to the library.

"Well, we had a very successful day," my aunt said throwing herself in a chair.

"So I see, Margaret. What on earth is all this? Surely it's not *all* for Ella to wear?"

"No of course not. Pierre had a rather cunning idea while we were out and much of it is for him."

"Oh?" I asked slowly and with some apprehension.

"Mais oui!" he said, eyes dancing with excitement. "I intend to forge the painting of Colonel Summerfield."

"But why?"

"Because, my dear Elspeth, you are going to return it to the art school and from there we will see where it goes."

"But can't we just use the one Edward did for me originally?"

I shook my head. "It's been damaged. They would notice straight away."

"Precisement!" Pierre said. "It would be too dangerous for then they would know that we know what they are doing."

I smiled at Pierre's rather convoluted way of explaining.

"Oh, yes of course," mother said. "But who is left at the school to give it to? Clementine and Monsieur Valin are no longer there."

"Rest assured someone will have taken Valin's place," Aunt Margaret said. "There are still too many valuable canvasses on the premises, including I suspect those currently being painted over in all innocence by your fellow students. They are unlikely to abandon such a valuable cover as the art school, plus of course they couldn't do so quickly without raising suspicion. But we won't send you alone, Elspeth; Gaston will accompany you."

"Yes all right, I'll do it." She moved to the sideboard to pour us all a drink and I made myself comfortable on the settee.

"I think we ought to return all of them," I said. "We are risking too much by them being here. We know whoever is behind this organisation is suspicious of us by the break-in and they are deadly serious. Just look at what has happened so far: three disappearances, a murder and a burglary. In my opinion it's just too dangerous to keep them, whereas if they were returned to the art school then at least we will be safe for the time being."

My aunt looked at me thoughtfully, and then glanced at Pierre who returned her look and nodded slowly. "Ella is correct," she said. "It's simply not worth jeopardising our lives for the sake of a few paintings, no matter how rare and significant they are. We will still have proof if we need it in the form of the Bruegel. Pierre can remove it to somewhere safe and Elspeth can return the others including the copy of the colonel's."

We all agreed to this plan with much relief.

"How long will it take for you to paint another version of the colonel's, Pierre?" I asked.

"One day!"

"Goodness, will it really?" exclaimed my mother. "It took Edward nearly two weeks."

"But he is not a professional, not by a long way," he replied, scowling at the picture as though affronted by its very existence. "I will begin in the morning at first light. I shall have this as my studio and use the settee to sleep. It would normally take a little time to dry but I have a way to expedite this process so it will be ready to return in three days. Now to the unveiling of the disguise!"

I sighed as Pierre pounced on a box and, lifting the lid, brought forth a plain dark beige linen suit, which would have struggled to have been fashionable even fifteen years before.

"We very nearly went with the sackcloth," Aunt Margaret said with unconcealed mirth.

"Oh and this is so much better," I said sardonically, lifting the dress by its shoulders. It was quite high on the neck with a lace collar, which when new would have been a light cream shade but now had aged to the colour of old tea. The sleeves came to just below the elbow and were finished by a turned up cuff fraying at the edge. It was drop-waisted, below which were two saggy pockets that no amount of careful pressing could return to their original shape, and lengthwise came to just above my ankle. I struggled to find even one redeeming factor.

The jacket was not much better. Fashioned from the same material it was collarless and quite shapeless, made only slightly less so by the belt to tie around my middle. I just knew I was going to look like a sack of potatoes. Thick beige hosiery and sensible, low-heeled brown shoes were next, and to top it all off a very sad-looking plain straw hat.

"Well, you've outdone yourself, Aunt Margaret," I said, and then hearing a peculiar noise behind me I found her and my mother clutching at each other in absolute fits of laughter while desperately trying to be quiet.

I looked back at Pierre who was equally amused and smiled.

"But there is more," he said thrusting a round box into my hands and removing the lid. "Eh voila!"

I dropped the box in surprise. "Is it dead?"

There was a roar of laughter from behind me. "Oh, Ella," my aunt said wiping her eyes. "You are absolutely priceless, darling. It's a wig."

"Well you could have warned me," I said, stooping to retrieve the contents and lifting it gingerly from the box. It was indeed a wig, straw coloured and unfortunately with a similar texture, and pinned up in an Edwardian style with a band of curl across the fringe.

"Gosh I really will be unrecognisable in this lot."

"There is one more addition," my aunt said.

"I really can't wait," I replied.

"Here you are." She handed me a pair of round, thick and heavy spectacles with a tortoiseshell frame. "They have been fitted with clear lenses so shouldn't affect your ability to see at all."

Finally there was a worn leather satchel containing a notepad and pencils.

"So who am I to be?"

"You are to be my assistant-cum-secretary, English of course, very shy, quiet and reserved. You will simply blend into the background and therefore will be able to see everything and take notes without being obvious."

"Yes, that it is a good cover. And what am I to be called?"

"We thought perhaps Miss Brown?"

I laughed and glanced at all the accoutrements. There was but one palette. "Yes, that will do nicely. Very apt indeed!"

Chapter TWELVE

THE NEXT MORNING AFTER BREAKFAST, with Pierre ensconced in the library having issued strict instructions not to disturb him, and my aunt up at the hotel telephoning to make an appointment for us to visit the Castille Company, mother and I decided to try out my disguise. We needed somebody to fool and Adele was the perfect choice. She'd seen me every day as myself so if I could make her believe I was Miss Brown then others would take it for granted.

It seemed my aunt had thought of everything as among the purchases we had discovered a light-coloured face powder and a pair of cream lace gloves. Having spent so many days in the glorious Riviera sunshine my skin had turned to a glowing honey colour, which would be an immediate betrayal. As Miss Brown, newly arrived from mostly soggy

England, I would naturally be pale, and the powder worked perfectly for my face and neck, with the gloves cleverly concealing my hands.

Next came the dreaded hosiery.

"Do you know, mother, I really don't think I can wear these, they are just so thick and itchy. I'll be driven quite mad in this heat."

"I'm sure I have something more suitable, dear. And let's face it they will hardly be seen."

Disappearing into her dressing room she emerged a moment later with a pair in a similar colour but much softer and of a lighter weight.

"Oh yes, these are perfect. Now let's put the rest of the ensemble together."

After half an hour of tweaking I was ready to face Adele as my alter ego.

"So what do you think?" I asked my mother as I put on the spectacles.

She came forward and unpinning the hat, adjusted its angle to fall a little more forward over my brow and fastened it in place.

"That's better. In all honesty even though you are my daughter, Ella, I truly hardly recognise you. It's quite disturbing."

I laughed. "Well, hopefully we can dupe your maid. If you check the coast is clear I'll nip outside and ring the bell."

"But what about your voice, darling, she's bound to recognise it?"

I flung myself in a chair. "Oh what a fool I am, of course she will. But what on earth can I do about it?"

"What about an accent of some sort. Scottish or Irish perhaps?"

"I'll try."

And try I did, but after ten minutes it was apparent I was quite hopeless. The problem was I didn't really know what either of those accents sounded like; I needed something to copy with which I was familiar and said as much to my mother.

"Well, let us first establish what Miss Brown is like. Pierre and Margaret both said she was shy and quiet so we should start there."

"Yes, she's more of a wallflower type I would imagine, terribly efficient at her job but lacking any basic social skills."

"She reminds me of that young girl who used to work at your father's factory, oh what was her name? Can you recall who I mean? When we used to open the house on Boxing Day for the staff Christmas party, she was always the one stood in a corner speaking quietly with a friend but never dancing or joining in. Dorothy, was it?"

"Dottie! Yes that's exactly who Miss Brown would sound like with flattened vowels of the north and her whispering voice."

"And don't forget the slight lisp."

I closed my eyes and tried to recall Dottie from when I was a child. It wasn't perfect but it didn't have to be; as long as I had a framework on which to hang the character it would work. I began to speak in a soft Yorkshire accent, emphasising the lisp every so often and not meeting my mother's eyes. The longer I practiced the more I felt Miss Brown emerge until I was satisfied I could fool Adele into thinking I was someone else.

"That was exceptionally good, Ella, well done."

"Now comes the real test," I said and after checking we were alone I ventured downstairs and quietly left the villa.

Standing outside the door to the villa, lace-clad finger poised over the bell, I was surprised to find how nervous I was. I took a deep breath, clutched my satchel to my chest like a shield and rang the bell. A moment later it was opened by the butler.

"Bonjour, Mademoiselle."

"Hello," I said in my soft whispering voice. "Miss Brown for Mr DuPont."

The butler indicated I should wait in the hall and disappeared into the villa. A moment later Adele appeared.

"Please this way, Mademoiselle Brown," she said and turned on her heel.

I followed meekly behind until we reached the drawing room where my mother had been waiting impatiently.

Adele curtsied. "Mademoiselle Brown for Monsieur DuPont, Madame."

"Thank you, Adele. Miss Brown, welcome, we've been expecting you. Mr DuPont is in the library if you'd like to follow me."

I nodded and said a quiet thank you.

"Shall I make up a room, Madame?" Adele asked.

Mother gave me an enquiring glance and I shook my head. "No thank you. Mr DuPont has arranged a room at the hotel for me."

Adele gave a curtsy then left the room. There had been absolutely no indication of recognition, she hadn't suspected a thing! We reached the library door and mother knocked once then opened it. "Mr DuPont, Miss Brown has arrived."

Pierre came to the door dressed in a paint-splattered smock, which hung to his knees, and a black beret perched over his right ear.

"Miss Brown? Yes! Miss Brown, at last, I was expecting you two days ago. Come in, come in, we have work to do."

I shared a smile with mother and we entered the library, closing the door behind us.

"Magnificent!" Pierre announced after I had said a few words and he had scrutinised every inch of my costume. "And the voice is completely correct."

Just then we heard my aunt. "Hello. Where is everybody?"

Mother opened the library door. "In here, Margaret. Miss Brown has just arrived."

"Has she indeed? Well, well."

I gave her a brief nod and said what a pleasure it was to meet her at last.

"Absolutely outstanding, darling, you're a natural. Down to the speech and the mannerisms you are completely in character," my aunt said. Then turning to Pierre, "We could have done with her in the Balkan's in twenty-two, don't you think?"

"Ah yes, the perfect governess!"

I shook my head. "I have no idea what you're talking about and know better than to ask, but I fooled the staff which was the objective. This gives me hope for the appointment at Castille's."

"Yes, there's success on that front too. You both have an appointment with the manager Monsieur Tremblay in three days' time. This will give Elspeth the chance to return the paintings. How are you getting on, Pierre?"

"It is almost finished it is a very simple picture. Tonight it will be unveiled. Now leave me in peace to continue."

※

The day finally came when my mother was to return the three paintings to the art school. Pierre had done an exceptional job with the forgery, so much so that even side-by-side none of us could tell which was the original. He had also changed the two mother had done herself, slightly altering the perspective; this would give her the excuse as to why she was bringing them back. There was also an additional secret regarding these two pieces of art but I wouldn't find out about it until much later.

I had decided to accompany her as my alter ego, for while I had practiced at the villa I really felt Miss Brown needed an outing in public. It was a risk but a small one, and I believed the benefits would outweigh the small possibility of danger should I been seen at both the art school and Castille's. If I played my character properly I should not really be noticed, and naturally in the light of Pierre DuPont's greatness I would fade into insignificance.

At mid morning we found ourselves in the rear of Pierre's limousine being driven by Gaston. Gaston himself was not dressed as a chauffeur however; he had an additional job once we arrived at the school.

"Are you nervous, dear?" my mother asked.

"Yes, I am rather. It's all very well swanning about the villa and fooling the staff, but I need to know I can keep in character for a good length of time and in an unfamiliar situation. I can't risk giving the game away when we're touring the factory, but I need to be vigilant and keep my eye open for anything that will give us a tangible clue."

"Darling, the onus isn't purely on you, you know, there are others working to solve this case. Have you heard from Captain Robillard at all?"

"Not yet, he may still be in Lyon and he is obviously distrustful of the telephone. I'm sure he'll be in touch when he knows something."

If I was being honest with myself I was feeling very put out about the lack of contact from Jacques. He'd promised to keep me updated at each step yet I had heard nothing, and regardless of what I had told my mother there were ways he could have got word to me.

We parked two streets away so as not to draw any unwanted attention and mother and I walked the remainder of the way carrying the pictures, leaving Gaston to make his own journey. We would meet back at the motor car once our separate business was concluded.

I had been correct about the hosiery, even now wearing a much lighter pair the mid-morning heat was becoming almost unbearable, attired as I was in several layers. I had always been under the impression ladies, if they did so at all, perspired in a gentle, barely perceptible and purely feminine way. Sadly this was not true in my case and I thought longingly of the cool waters of the ocean while slowly turning into a wet rag.

After ten minutes we entered the school and made our way to the amateur studio where we found another teacher, unknown to my mother, setting up for the day's students. We'd arrived deliberately early so as not to encounter anyone mother knew, thus avoiding questions about Edward, particularly as we were returning his canvas. I remained shyly in the background but within hearing distance while my mother spoke to him in English.

"Good morning, I am Mrs Bridges, a student here, I've come to return some paintings."

"I see, and are they yours, Madame?"

"Two of them are but I've realised they need a little more work, see here and here," she pointed to the sections Pierre had altered. "The perspective is quite wrong, isn't it? Such a silly mistake, I'm really rather annoyed with myself. But they are gifts and I do so want them to be right. I'd like to put them in the store room and come back when my guests have returned home. I shall then send them on by post when I have finished them."

"Of course, Madame, I will arrange it. And the third? It is this one, yes? And you say it does not belong to you?"

"That's not what I meant. It does belong to me but I did not paint it, it was a gift."

"Ah, and now you do not want this gift?"

"Not any longer."

"It was done here at the school?"

"Yes, by Colonel Summerfield, he was a student here too. However he has now apparently left and I doubt he will be returning. I wouldn't know considering he hasn't been in touch, but I certainly have no wish to keep it. So if you could take it back, another student could perhaps re-use it?"

"Thank you, Madame, I will put it in the store along with the others. Au revoir."

Mother said goodbye and we retraced our steps.

"How was that?" she asked me quietly.

"Perfect. You struck the right balance between being aggrieved, resentful, upset and angry. There's no doubt he believed every word you said and I'm sure he'll pass the message on to whoever is in charge."

As we made our way out of the school grounds, we spied Gaston lounging against the wall beneath the open window of the office where we had overheard Valin's conversation. His eyes flicked our way briefly but he ignored us, all concentration upon rolling a cigarette, and dressed as a student he blended in perfectly. All we had to do now was return to the motor car, await his return and hope he had learned something.

Chapter THIRTEEN

THE APPOINTMENT MY AUNT HAD MADE for us with Monsieur Tremblay was at half past three in the afternoon, which would give us two hours before the manager left for the day and the evening staff took over. Apparently the factory worked around the clock in two shifts, and I wondered at both the amount and type of work a business such as this would have, that it required a twenty-four hour schedule. I voiced my opinion to Pierre who astutely pointed out it was likely the legitimate work was done during the day, and the more nefarious dealings happened at night. I realized that should we discover anything unusual a secret nocturnal visit would be necessary.

"By the way, you did very well yesterday, Gaston, excellent initiative to find the recipient of the telephone call."

"Merci, Monsieur DuPont."

I smiled at Pierre's praise of Gaston; he deserved it as he really had done an exceptional job. Apparently, no sooner had mother and me left the school, the tutor had rushed into the office and made a telephone call. Situated as he was beneath the open window, Gaston had managed to hear the conversation and relayed it to us when we met him back at the motor car.

The tutor had told whomever he had spoken to that mother had just returned all three paintings, including the one Edward had done. The tutor had also mentioned something about *doing it in his lunch hour tomorrow*, meaning today.

But the part we were all so impressed with was when Gaston had entered the office and asked the telephone operator to transfer him to the number just used; it had been answered by a secretary at Castille Art and Antiques. We now knew for certain the business was involved.

"We're getting awfully close to solving this mystery I feel, Pierre," I said. "I just hope we are not falling into some kind of trap by visiting today. We know the business is involved so why not wait and go back at night when the illegal side of things is going on?"

"We will of course, my dear, but today is all about reconnaissance. We cannot go in blind or we *will* find ourselves in a trap. Today we get the lay of the land and gather as much pertinent information as we can, that way when we go back at night we are better prepared to succeed in our objective."

"Do we know anything at all about these premises?" I asked. "I assume you have done some research already?"

Pierre chuckled, "Of course, and Maggie has also been working behind the scenes but information is scarce, what we do know is the site is vast. It was a former textile factory for the garment industry and consists of several large warehouses, although not all of them are in use now."

"I see. And is there more than one entrance?"

"Astute as ever, Ella; yes I'm sure there must be and it's crucial we find out, but the only one we are sure of is the one we will use today."

"Well I have my note-book; I'll make a plan as we go. I assume with a company this size there are offices?"

"Indeed, the front of the business is quite obvious, with the main building housing the foyer and offices. It's the part at the rear we need to gather more information on. What we can surmise is, during its previous incarnation there would have been several loading bays. This would have been where the raw material was delivered and the final product, the cloth, once manufactured, was loaded and delivered to the customer."

"It's very likely then that there is at least one other entrance, the behind the scenes working part, if you like," I said.

"Yes, I agree. Nowadays it is fine art, furniture and antiques which are the product," Pierre continued. "Some restoration work is done there as well as the production of art materials for the various retailers. All in all it is rather a hotchpotch of services."

"Perhaps so but it is very clever to hide an illegal business behind a legitimate one."

"And I suspect it is more common than one would suppose. Well, let us see what we can discover to our advantage, my dear. If nothing else it should be an interesting visit."

***

I was extremely grateful that my aunt when making the appointment had insisted on it being a low-key and private visit, for we were greeted at the door by numerous members of the office staff, bowing and curtsying as though it were a royal occasion, the only thing absent was a red carpet. Goodness knows what we would have had to contend with on a formal visit, a marching band and an unveiling of a statue of Pierre perhaps.

Monsieur Tremblay was overly effusive in his greeting of Pierre, and babbled delightedly in French as he escorted us to his office. Once there at Pierre's request he reverted to English so I was able to understand, but very quickly, as we had hoped, once the brief introductions were made

I was forgotten, seated as I was in the shadow of the great man himself.

Over an excellent afternoon tea which would have fed at least half the workforce, Pierre regaled Monsieur Tremblay with humorous anecdotes of his more daring escapades as an artist and his rise to international fame. Pierre was at his sparkling best and the manager was thoroughly entertained, although I doubted the veracity of the stories. Eventually with tea finished Pierre got down to business, and Monsieur Tremblay, safe in the knowledge he was now a trusted friend and a part of Pierre's innermost circle, was happy to oblige in any request.

We left the manager's office, headed down a flight of stairs at the rear and through an external door, leading to a criss-cross of roads giving access to the large buildings, it was almost a small village in itself and immediately I made a start on my plan. As we approached the first building Pierre asked Monsieur Tremblay more about the business.

"It is a family affair this business, Tremblay?"

"Non, non, Monsieur DuPont, it is Monsieur Armand Castille who owns the business only. But he has employed his nephew, Louis Castille, in this last year."

"In what capacity?"

"To find and acquire new business," the manager sighed. "He is on a vacation at present but if you would prefer to deal with him then..."

"Mais non, my friend, it was simply curiosity. He is successful?"

Tremblay shrugged. "He is young."

"Ah, I understand. The youth of today they are more interested in parties and being seen than the work, no?"

"Oui! That is it exactly. Do you know the first new business he secured?" Pierre shook his head as Tremblay moved in closer and dropped his voice. "Donating canvases to art schools. Giving them away, you understand? What is the point of giving them away? It makes no money for the company. But who am I to say such a thing, I am merely an employee."

Pierre's eyes met mine briefly and I nodded. This was the link we had been looking for but Tremblay had said art schools in the plural and there were many in France. It looked as though the fraud was far greater than we had realised. Louis Castille had also just become my number one suspect.

"Ah, do not worry, my friend, who are we to question the wisdom of these businessmen? Perhaps there is method in their madness but let us not concern ourselves with these trifles. It is the art we believe in, non?"

"You are a wise man, Monsieur DuPont. Now through here is the furniture restoration department..."

We passed through a door into a vast warehouse split into three sections where the overriding smell was one of wood shavings, turpentine and beeswax, and the noise of lathes, band-saws and sanding machines made conversation almost impossible. As we moved through the sections it became quieter and in the last one we found a dozen specialist French polishers and cabinet makers putting finishing touches to a range of exceptional furniture. According to Tremblay the majority of the pieces were either destined for sale in the showrooms owned by Armand Castille or already sold to buyers abroad. The rest were private commissions undertaken on behalf of the owners.

The second large building was where the manufacturing of art materials took place: pencils, paint brushes, palettes and easels were all in various stages of assembly, and the latter end was taken up with the making and stretching of canvases. I looked at them closely while Pierre continued to discuss fictitious business matters with Tremblay but could see no sign of any hidden masters; we needed to look elsewhere.

Leaving this building, we walked across a central square to the other side where warehouse number three was waiting.

"I think you will find this section most interesting, Monsieur DuPont," Tremblay said. "It is where the restoration of the paintings takes place."

"Yes indeed, I am looking forward to this part very much."

The restoration consisted again of three main areas, and Pierre was in his element. I, on the other hand was becoming increasingly frustrated at our lack of findings.

Realistically, I knew the earliest we could do anything would be under cover of darkness tonight, and that was assuming we found a reason to do so. But it didn't stop my impatience from rising to the surface, and it took a huge amount of will for me not to shout out loud, 'Let's get on with it!'

So while Pierre and Tremblay discussed how the four skilled artists restored the paintings, and the half dozen specialists made moulds for missing sections of ornate swept frames, and gilded them by hand no less! I wandered passed the antique stretcher restorers toward the back of the building.

Here was where the finished items were being carefully packaged for delivery, and a familiar movement caught my eye.

Weaving in and out of the stacked frames, his black tail flicking while his green eyes stared at me unblinkingly, was Phantom. Once he was assured of my attention he stalked gracefully to a batch of paintings waiting to be packed and sent to their owners, and among them were three that I recognised immediately. At last!

I quickly wrote a message and tore it out of my notebook. Folding it in half I hurried to Pierre, who was still talking animatedly to a frame restorer, and slid it into his hand. He scanned it quickly and slipped it into his pocket.

"It has been most interesting, merci beaucoup. Now, Monsieur Tremblay, perhaps the next building? It is for packaging of the art materials you said, yes?"

"Oui, the final step in the production. This way please."

We followed behind the manager, giving us a chance to quickly talk. My brief note to Pierre informed him I had discovered both mother's and the colonel's paintings ready for dispatch.

"Pierre, Castille's are behind this racket," I whispered furiously. "But our only evidence is about to disappear. We have to come back tonight!"

"I agree, now they have what they think is the Bruegel, Colonel Summerfield's safety net has been eliminated."

"They will kill him, Pierre. I only hope they haven't done so already. I need to complete my map; can you make an excuse to Tremblay for me to stay outside?"

"Of course, but be quick with your sketch, I don't know how long I will be inside. Packaging is most boring."

Citing my feminine weakness, much to my chagrin until I realised how perfectly in my character it was, Pierre explained to Monsieur Tremblay I would remain outside in the fresh air while he toured the packing area.

Once they were inside I set to scurrying around the site and making additions to my map. To my dismay there was a high wall around the entire perimeter, I couldn't imagine how we'd get over that.

As well as the four large warehouses we had toured, there were numerous smaller outbuildings, and a large garage housing a fleet of delivery vehicles with the company logo. At the end of the area, which essentially cut the plot into two halves I came to a chain link fence, the gates of which were padlocked, and beyond another series of warehouses mirroring the layout of the ones where I stood. These were in poor condition with broken windows, many of which were boarded up, missing roof tiles and an air of dereliction, but it was the translucent figure leaning against one of the walls which captured my attention, it was the late Monsieur Armand Castille himself.

This was it! There must be something important about this particular warehouse, why else would he be here? I clasped my hands through the fence and peered at the warehouse door in the distance. Yes there! It was supposedly derelict but on the door was a brand new padlock glinting in the sunshine. I would bet my hat that's where they were keeping Edward.

I made a note of the building on my plan and quickly returned to the packaging warehouse where I found Pierre and the manager just departing. Our reconnaissance was complete and had gone without a hitch. The next stage would be far more dangerous.

Once we arrived back at the villa I dashed upstairs to my room and removed all traces of Miss Brown, before venturing downstairs to join the others in the library. It was absolute bliss to remove the layers of clothing and exchange them for a cool cotton dress.

"Pierre has just been telling us you played your part beautifully, Ella," my mother said.

"Oh yes, right down to a mild attack of the vapours the weaker sex are so prone to," I replied with a smile.

"Not all of us, dear," my aunt said. "Now what did you learn? Pierre wouldn't breathe a word until you arrived."

I turned to the page in my notebook where I had drawn the plan of the premises, "This is the layout of the property and buildings. Now mother took the paintings back yesterday and from what we can elicit from the one-sided telephone conversation Gaston overheard, they were due to be delivered to Castille's at lunchtime today. I can confirm this was the case, I saw them there myself waiting to be sent on."

"Goodness, they didn't waste any time, did they?" mother said.

"No they didn't, which worries me. I feel now the window of opportunity in which to find the colonel has just shrunk considerably." I gave my mother a concerned glance but she was already thinking the same way.

"They have no reason to keep him alive now they have

what they want, do they? That's assuming he is still alive."

"Which is why Pierre and I have decided to go back tonight when it's dark."

"So soon? Yes of course you must but not alone surely, what about the police?"

"I don't know who to trust except Jacques. Of course I will write to him and explain everything but either you or Aunt Margaret will have to deliver it to his villa. You'll need to apprise Beecher too; he is I think more than a simple butler and is privy to much of what Jacques is involved in. If Jacques has not yet returned from Lyon then he will be able to help in his stead I'm sure."

"We will both go," my aunt said, getting an agreeing nod from mother.

"My visit will be in the newspapers tomorrow also," Pierre said ruefully. "We caught the flash of the camera bulbs as we were leaving. Reporters are a tenacious breed and connections will be made between us all soon if they have not done so already, so..." He gave a shrug.

"It will be easy for them too considering we all travelled here together," my aunt said. "All right, what is the plan and what can we do to help?"

We decided to leave at half past nine, a little under three hours hence, which would get us to the site at approximately ten o'clock. Gaston would drive us in his own motor car, much smaller, less ostentatious and far more practical than the limousine, and mother and Aunt Margaret would arrange a taxi to take them to Jacques with my message. Pierre was of the opinion that whatever the gang had planned would take place in the early hours of the following morning, thus reducing their chance of discovery, but just in case he had underestimated them we needed to be in place as soon as possible and attempt to locate the colonel if he was there. It was going to be a long night.

"We will need dark clothing, practical and comfortable," Pierre said, and from his tone I knew he had experienced this sort of thing before. "Do you have such a thing?"

I nodded. I had brought with me a pair of dark grey slacks, and teamed with a long sleeved button down linen shirt in black borrowed from my mother, and a pair of my own dark beach shoes, I was set.

"Ella, give me the map you made," said Pierre. "I will make copies; it would be prudent to all have our own in the event we are split up. We will also need torches."

"I can help with those," my mother said. "There are occasions when the electric power is cut here so I always have several on hand."

It didn't take long for Pierre to duplicate my plan and when we were all holding individual copies I went through it in more detail.

"The plot itself is in essence split into two sections by a chain link fence with a central gate which is padlocked.

The first half is the working part where we toured, the second looks derelict but there were some indications it was in use, although not for the legitimate side of the business I'd wager. This particular building..." I indicated the warehouse where Armand Castille had appeared to me. "...I believe is the important one and where we should concentrate our initial search. Access to the derelict part is through a gate from a road running opposite to and parallel with the main entrance."

"Is there a guard?" my aunt asked.

"I didn't see one but that doesn't mean he was not there. In fact I doubt they would leave the place unguarded, there's too much money at stake, so let's assume there is. The tricky part will be how to get in, the surrounding walls are too high to climb and the gates I did see were locked. Any ideas?"

"What are these here?" Pierre asked, indicating a series of oblongs I had pencilled in along the East wall. The main entrance to the derelict section, opposite the South entrance we had come through when touring, was along the North side.

"Out-buildings. Probably used for storage at some point. Why?"

Pierre drummed his fingers on the table for some minutes while deep in thought. None of us interrupted. At last he spoke, "Eh Voila! I have at least two, possibly three ways of entering."

"Would you care to share?" Aunt Margaret asked in sardonic tones.

"Of course, they are like this..."

Pierre explained in detail what his ideas were and while they seemed faintly preposterous and far removed from anything I had done before, they were in fact eminently possible. We spent an hour or so going over the finer detail, then Pierre left with Gaston to exchange the car, change his clothes and pick up some tools he would need. I wrote a long explanatory letter to Jacques, care of Beecher, then went to get changed myself. Goodness knows what would happen but we had to see it through. I fervently hoped for success and prayed the ending would be a happy one for all concerned, especially Colonel Summerfield.

Chapter FOURTEEN

◈

AT NINE THIRTY ON THE DOT, with my mother and Aunt Margaret already in a taxi en route to Jacques villa, Pierre and I commenced our journey with Gaston at the wheel to what I hoped would be our last visit to Castille's Arts and Antiques.

The entire plot was circumnavigated by a dirt track road and Gaston parked on the East side next to where we had estimated the row of out-buildings were.

"Right, to the roof!" Pierre said.

"I can't believe I am doing this," I hissed, crawling up the boot of the motor car and crouching on the roof.

"It is fun, Ella."

"No Pierre. Swimming in the ocean is fun. Building sandcastles is fun. Climbing on top of a high wall from the roof of a motor car, then dropping down onto old sheds whose roofs we don't know if we can rely on, in the dark, is terrifying."

Pierre chuckled. "Where is your sense of adventure?"

"I left it back at the villa. Why can't we use the ladder in the boot?"

"Because they are a special extendable design and will take too long to set up. Now reach for Gaston's hand and he will pull you onto the wall."

I took a deep breath and on shaking legs stood up. I could just make out Gaston's silhouette lying atop the wall and groped blindly for the hand I knew was waiting. Eventually I grasped it tightly and with a sudden lurch was lifted into the air.

I scrabbled up the side of the wall with my feet, to help Gaston, and a split second later was lying on top of the wall, my breath ragged and heart pounding.

"Are you all right, Mademoiselle?" Gaston whispered in my ear.

I jumped, I hadn't realised he was so close. "Yes, I think so."

"You need to get down now; I have to bring up Monsieur DuPont. Give me your hands and move your legs over the side, I will lower you down."

"Dear god, this is horrible."

"Don't worry I will not let you go until you are safely on the roof below. It will only be a matter of a foot, no more. But we must be quick! Be brave Mademoiselle." He said with urgency.

I was suddenly hit with a desire to laugh and had to swallow the rising hysteria. Clasping Gaston's hands tightly I maneuvered my legs over the side of the wall, whimpering slightly as I did so, and let him take my whole weight. I was now dangling freely. Suddenly he let go and I was dropping. A split second later I was on top of the shed. I'd made it! And the shed roof hadn't caved in!

I moved to one side while the process was repeated with Pierre, then we were scrambling from the out-building roof and down to the ground. We crouched side by side in the shadows for a moment to catch our breaths while Gaston, having jumped effortlessly back down the other side, moved the car to a more secluded spot.

"What would we have done if Gaston had not been so strong?"

"Used the ladder of course."

Of course.

The ground where we had come to rest was halfway between two of the large warehouses, and I estimated we had at least two hundred yards to navigate before we reached the one to our left where I had seen the apparition of Armand Castille. I grabbed Pierre's arm and whispered, "The one we want is to our left. I think it best we keep to the wall until we are as near as possible then make a dash for it."

Pierre agreed with me, the only problem lay in the fact it was almost pitch black and we could barely see a foot in front of our faces.

"I can't see a thing! I wish we could use the torches."

"Me also, but we can't risk it, what if the light is seen?"

"Well, stay close behind me."

Gingerly with my left hand on the wall I began to make slow progress forward with Pierre doing the same. It was an interminable journey and more than once I came upon a large obstacle, a relic from the days when the site was a textile factory.

"Ow!" I said, stopping so suddenly that Pierre crashed into me.

"What is it?"

"I stubbed my toe."

"Your toe?" he said wheezing with giggles.

I held my hand out in front of me and instantly hit a large iron construction; wide, high and rusty, with sharp bits sticking out at various angles. "I was lucky not to break my nose! And stop laughing."

We skirted round it carefully, and had just reached a stack of old disused pallets no more than half a dozen yards from our destination when Pierre grabbed my arm and dragged me behind them.

Seconds later two men appeared with lowered torches. Lighting cigarettes they chatted quietly.

I slapped a hand over my mouth to stifle the scream rising in my throat. Something furry with a tail had run over my foot. A whispered expletive told me Pierre had felt the same.

The pallets were stacked haphazardly and we had a small but clear line of sight to the men. And on such a still night we could hear every word.

After what seemed like hours but was probably no more than ten minutes, I was becoming excruciatingly uncomfortable but dared not move. If we were discovered the game would be up and I was positive at that point we would be joining Armand Castille. Just as the cramp was beginning to set in I heard a name which put it out of my mind completely. Even in quickly spoken French I recognised it and grabbed Pierre's arm in surprise. I felt sure my shock was mirrored in his face because the name we had heard was Perret. The detective who had dismissed so easily my mother's concerns regarding her missing friend, and who had the audacity to intimate her arrest was involved in this rapacity up to his eyeteeth!

I quietly seethed, imminent cramp forgotten, as I waited for the two men to depart. As soon as they disappeared back inside the building I hissed at Pierre, "Did you hear that? Perret is involved!"

"I heard, Ella. But this is the least of our problems."

"Why? What else did they say?"

"Perret will be here in an hour or so. Monsieur Valin and Colonel Summerfield are both inside, alive but barely. They have been severely beaten and tortured."

I suddenly found I couldn't breathe. This was appalling news.

"That is not all. If they are still alive when Perret arrives they are to be killed immediately and the bodies disposed of. Ella, we do not have long."

"Pierre, we need to get in there now but how are we to get them both out? If they are so very injured then any movement could kill them."

"Do you have your notebook and pencil as we arranged?"

"Yes, here."

"Switch on your torch but shade it with your hand. It is time to write to Gaston."

I did as Pierre asked and watched as he wrote a quick but succinct message in French for his driver, and then wrapped it around a piece of wood broken from a pallet.

"Here take this and throw it over the wall where we came over. Gaston will be waiting for it and will give you a sign he has received it."

"What sort of sign?"

"You will know it but it will not be verbal in case he raises the alarm of those inside. Now use your torch but carefully, point it to the ground and hurry back we don't have much time. I'll wait for you here."

I was in a heightened state of terror as I ran back to the out-buildings, with adrenaline coursing through my body and the blood rushing in my ears, and every step I took on a broken piece of glass sounded like a pistol crack. I was panic stricken in case the noise should alert one of the gang but dared not stop. Eventually I reached the out-buildings and switched off the torch. So far so good. No one had come out to investigate.

I could see the top of the wall dark black against the slightly lighter shade of the night sky and took several deep breaths to steady myself. Grasping one end of the wooden slat I prayed my skill on the school netball court years ago wouldn't fail me now. Swinging my arm over my shoulder I flung the wood as high as I could, and watched with great satisfaction as it sailed over the wall, coming to land on the opposite side with an audible but dull thud.

Seconds later I thought I heard a small cough although it was difficult to tell with my heart hammering so loudly, then a lighted cigarette came flying over the wall, it's orange tip glowing in the blackness, to land in a small shower of sparks a short distance away. I hoped this was Gaston's signal.

Turning the torch back on I started my return journey and a few minutes later the sound of a motor car on the other side of the wall made itself known. Gaston was leaving.

Eventually I crawled back into the space behind the pallets, nerves in shreds and breathing heavily.

"Well done, Ella. I heard Gaston drive past. How are you feeling?"

"A little shaky and I need to catch my breath but I am all right. What did you tell Gaston?"

"Three things; to contact his brothers and delay Perret's arrival here…"

"Only delay, not stop?"

"Yes. We need him here so we can catch him in the act to prove his culpability. He will deny everything otherwise."

"That's true. What are the other two things?"

"To get word to Captain Robillard and Beecher, and to inform the police here in Nice what is happening. Not all police are corrupt and we need to put our trust in someone."

"Yes I agree. So the plan is to enter the warehouse, find the colonel and Valin, and help them escape after we have subdued the members of the gang who are on guard inside?"

"Precisely."

"Come on then, let's go before I begin to panic at our lack of a real plan."

We carefully eased our way out of our hiding place and stood up, stretching cramped limbs. We paused for a while, listening, but all was silent. Then from around the corner of the building a barely perceptible but familiar black silhouette appeared.

"I don't know if the coast is clear as it were but we can waste no more time," Pierre whispered.

"It's clear."

"How do you know?"

"Do you remember when we first met while I was investigating the death of the vicar on Linhay?"

"Of course."

"You said at our meeting you thought I saw the world slightly differently sometimes. Well this is one of those times."

"Then lead on by all means, Ella. I shall follow and put my trust in your otherworldly guidance."

I took a deep breath and we cautiously followed Phantom into the building.

※

We bypassed the large double doors belonging to the loading bay and I watched as my ghostly companion walked through a small door at the side. Turning the handle I carefully pushed it open and cautiously peered inside, it was a long narrow hallway and much to my relief was empty. Pierre, close behind, gently shut the door and we pursued Phantom as he ascended the wooden staircase at the far end, ignoring a double width door which I assumed led to the ground floor.

The staircase consisted of two landings heading around

to the right in a similar way to a spiral staircase, and at the top a narrow platform with a plank floor and wooden balustrade took up the full width of the warehouse. A bank of apertures which once contained glass looked over the large ground floor of the warehouse proper, where the rusty skeletons of long dead machinery still stood casting malevolent shadows in the light of two small lamps. I looked at Pierre anxiously for in the pooling circles of light sat four men playing cards on an upturned box.

Another door at the far end of where we stood led out onto a metal gantry which was built around the whole of the outer circumference of the building, with six walkways at equal distances stretching from one side to the other. It was in the middle of the central walkway, directly above the guards, I noticed the cages.

No matter how awful I had thought our chance of success originally, it had now become impossible. For out of the three cages, two of them held a body.

I grabbed Pierre's arm and pulled him down into a crouch behind the solid section situated below the empty window frames.

"Pierre, this is impossible. The floor of the walkway is made up of grates, even if by some miracle we managed to be quiet while navigating rusty old metal we will be seen. And the cages are right above the guards!" I whispered.

"Turn on your torch," was the only answer I received.

"Why?"

"Quickly, I want to check the time."

Exasperated I did as he asked, then turned it off again at his nod.

"Now what?"

"Now we wait," he said.

"What on earth for, Pierre?"

But the words had no sooner left my lips than an almighty explosion assaulted my ears and rocked the building.

"That," he said.

"What is it?" I asked in horror.

"Our diversion. Gaston and his kin have arrived at the outer gates. Now let us proceed through the door to the gantry and make haste. The guards will be leaving below us imminently."

We scurried crablike to the end of the hall and opened the door. Once on the other side we stopped momentarily to watch the guards run to investigate the cacophony outside, and a second later we were charging down the gantry towards the middle walkway and the cages.

As I had thought the third cage was empty, but if the rust-coloured stains on the floor and bars were any indication, it had been recently occupied. To my utter dismay there were heavy padlocks on both cage doors, something else I hadn't thought of and I was becoming seriously frustrated at my own ineptitude.

"Pierre, they are locked! How are we going to free them?"

Once again I wondered at the former life of Pierre as he took from an inside pocket a small bright orange velvet roll with a purple tie, containing various lock picking instruments and deftly opened the padlocks. I turned to the one containing the colonel while Pierre ministered to Monsieur Valin. Both were bloodied and bruised and I suspected were suffering broken bones. I just hoped we could rouse them and they could walk.

I shook a shoulder. "Colonel Summerfield, can you hear me? Please wake up we're here to rescue you." There was no sign he had heard me and Pierre was also struggling to get a reaction from Valin. We shook them and cajoled several times but to no avail.

"Do you think they are drugged?" I asked.

"Possibly. Let me try this," he retrieved a small vial from his toolkit and removing the stopper wafted it under Valin's nose. Almost at once he opened his eyes, took a deep breath and began to cough and retch. Pierre handed me the smelling salts and I did the same to the colonel. Much to my relief he also began to cough.

"Oh thank heavens," I said.

"You have Maggie to thank for this idea."

The colonel had opened his one good eye the other was swollen shut, but gradually he began to focus.

"Elspeth?" he croaked out.

"Can you walk, Colonel? We need to get you out of here and we've not much time."

"Will try. Ribs broken and right arm."

Both men had had to endure a fetal position during their captivity as the cages were so small, consequently it took some time for their protesting limbs to begin to work. It was excruciatingly slow and with the clock ticking and the added complication of broken bones, it was a while before Valin and the colonel were out of their cages and upright. I grabbed the colonel around the waist and slinging his left arm over my shoulders we took a tottering step forward, Edward bent almost double favouring his broken ribs. It was in this way, step by faltering step we made it across the walkway to the main gantry, Pierre and Valin in similar shuffling style close behind. At the door we had entered onto the gantry we stopped to catch our breaths and took stock of our situation. To my mind escape was practically impossible but we had come too far to stop now.

"What is the plan, Pierre?" I asked.

"Now we exit through this door, go to the top of the staircase and wait. I suspect Gaston will be at the end of his little display very soon and the guards will return. We need to be ready to run down the stairs…"

"Run? Pierre, we can barely muster up a sedate trot with these two, how are we to run?"

"Then we just go as fast as possible! We need to be out

of the building and back to our hiding place behind the pallets before they discover their prisoners are missing."

There was no chance to discuss further the dangers of such a plan, not only because we didn't have another one but because at that moment everything went quiet outside. In the distance we heard several motor car doors slam, then the roaring of engines as they were driven away.

"Now!" said Pierre.

"Can we get to the bottom and hide underneath the staircase instead of waiting at the top?" I asked.

"It's a good idea that," said Pierre. "If we hurry yes we might just make it before the guards return."

I turned to the colonel. "Can you run?"

"I can try. I'm sorry, I see now you're not Elspeth."

"No. But I am her daughter and she is terribly worried about you."

For a moment his one good eye brightened and I saw renewed strength and determination in his countenance, then I opened the door and dragged him through as quickly as I could.

Hurrying to the staircase, we began to descend. At every step Edward grunted in pain as his ribs were jarred or his broken arm banged against the banister, but I couldn't afford to be gentle. If we were caught I had no doubt we would be killed. Eventually we arrived at the bottom just as I heard the laughter of the guards outside. Mere seconds after the four of us had squeezed into the cramped dark space under the stairs, the door opened and all four came in, laughing and jostling one another as they relived the action.

The minute they were through the door into the warehouse I spied Phantom at the far end of the hallway by the door waiting for us.

"Let's go!" I whispered and we hurried down the hall and through the door. Turning immediately right and aiming toward the perimeter wall whose shadow would give us added protection, we were halfway to the pallets when we heard shouts behind us. The guards had just realised their prisoners had escaped; luckily they started searching in the opposite direction. Picking up the pace we at last reached our hiding place where Pierre handed me his tool roll and told me to throw it over the wall, obviously a signal for Gaston.

"Quickly, in here," I said pushing the colonel toward the stack of wood.

Suddenly there was blinding light and half a dozen torches were aimed in our direction. We had been caught!

❖

"So near yet so far," the colonel said and slid down the wall, utterly exhausted, to land in a heap on the ground.

"It is not over yet, my friends, have a leetle faith," Pierre said quietly in the most astonishing and quite frankly to my mind, ridiculous display of positivity I had ever encountered. We were surrounded by gun-toting hoodlums and likely to be shot at any minute.

For a short while we all stared at each other in silence, then sauntering into the light came a swarthy-looking man, dreadfully attractive but with cold blue eyes utterly devoid of anything remotely sympathetic. It was as though we were mere specimens under his microscope and I realised then how very dangerous he was, for he was quite obviously emotionally unstable. There would be no reasoning with such a disturbed personality.

"Perret," the colonel croaked next to me.

I had known instinctively who he was but the confirmation of my thoughts must have somehow registered on my face because Perret immediately addressed me in English.

"I see you know who I am, Miss Bridges. Yes I am also aware of you and your... little pet," he said, eying Pierre with obvious disdain.

"You are nothing but a common murderer," I replied with a bravado I did not feel.

When I look back at my deliberate goading of him with those words it must have been sheer lunacy which made me speak, but at the time I thought one may as well be hanged for a sheep as a lamb.

His eyes glinted with momentary anger as he stepped

forward and lifted my chin with the tip of his ebony cane, an affectation I would have been amused at had I not been so afraid, "Hardly common. And be careful, Miss Bridges, I can make your death either quick or long-drawn out and very, very painful."

"Like you did with Clementine Dubois and Armand Castille?"

He cocked his head to one side and smiled coldly and I felt a rivulet of icy fear trickle down my back. "They were merely in the way. Nothing more than bugs to be squashed beneath my boot. You however interest me, Miss Bridges. I think I shall play with you for a while before I kill you."

And I thought if I were ever to come face to face with the devil he would look exactly like Perret.

Suddenly he thrust me back with his cane and turned to his men. "Take them to the cages."

The guards holstered their weapons and were advancing upon us when pandemonium broke out. Simultaneously several objects were lobbed over the wall resulting in loud bangs and copious amounts smoke, spotlights, which I had missed mounted on the buildings, were switched on, flooding the entire area in light, and several motor cars, sirens blaring, skidded to a halt in the road. I grabbed Pierre and hunkered down against the wall with Valin and the colonel as shots were fired and a bullet ricocheted off the wall not far from my ear.

Extendable ladders were dropped and Gaston, his brothers and to my amazement, Beecher, swarmed over the top of the wall to pounce on the guards, wrestling them to the ground. Shouts and yells could be heard from every direction over the top of the firecrackers Gaston had thrown, and I put my hands over my ears to deaden the noise. Suddenly and without warning there was silence, and the last thing I saw through the smoke and the haze before blackness overtook me, was Jacques handcuffing a prostrate Perret. We were safe.

Chapter FIFTEEN

I GROPED MY WAY BACK to consciousness moments later as a hand gently tapped my cheek and a cold damp cloth mopped my brow. I groaned and opened my eyes.

"Look, she's awake."

"Ella, can you hear me? Are you hurt? Can you sit up?"

I peered up at the two ancient hags, not understanding what I was seeing. "Who are you?"

"Oh good lord, she doesn't recognise us. Do you think she's lost her memory?"

"Don't be silly, Elspeth, we look like an amateur production of Macbeth. Ella, it's your aunt and your mother. Now are you hurt?"

I sat up and stared at them. "No, no I'm fine. I take it you were some sort of decoy? Well, the Weird Sisters was an inspired choice."

My aunt produced a most unladylike snort and rising to her feet declared, "She's fine. Now come along, dear, it's time to go home."

"How is Edward? What about Valin? And where is Pierre?"

"Pierre is talking with Gaston and the others have been taken to hospital. A few broken bones, bruises and a case of accidental concussion as far as Valin is concerned. I believe he tried to resist arrest, but they will make a full recovery. And I'm sure you'll be pleased to know Perret and his gang of vagabonds have been rounded up and thrown in gaol. Now home to bed for us all. We will have plenty of time to discuss all the finer details tomorrow."

❖

A combination of not getting to bed until the early hours, and being so utterly exhausted now the adrenaline had left my system meant I had slept a deep dream-free sleep for a full eight hours, and didn't wake until late morning. By the time I was ready and downstairs it was after midday but I still found mother, my aunt, Pierre and Jacques having lunch on the verandah and marvelled how everyone but me needed so little sleep. Official statements from us all would be needed later but over lunch we discussed the case and our individual parts in it as friends.

"How is the colonel, mother?"

"I have just returned from visiting him in the hospital and he is doing much better. His ribs have been strapped and his broken arm set, and he's been given something for the pain which has helped no end. He was mortified to think he had put me in so much danger by gifting me his painting, but he had no idea of the scale of the operation until he was caught and it was too late."

"Did he tell them he had given the painting to you?"

"He never breathed a word; even after all they did to him he tried to keep me safe. He suspects they burgled my villa as a last resort; they had looked everywhere else apparently. He asked me to apologise to you all."

"There's no need, he wasn't to know," I said. "So what is his name? We can't continue calling him Edward Summerfield."

"It's William Fitzwater. He's of Irish descent."

I nodded. "And what of Valin?" I asked the table at large but Jacques answered.

"He was formally arrested as you know, then taken to hospital where he remains under police guard. He too will make a full recovery. I spent most of the night taking his statement, and it's quite apparent he had got himself in far deeper than he'd wanted and ran, in fear for his life. He had accrued severe gambling debts and saw this scheme initially as a way of making money; however the murder of Madame Dubois was too much. Unluckily for him he was caught almost at once by Perret's men and imprisoned at the Castille warehouse."

"Armand Castille is also most likely dead," I said, even though I knew it to be true I couldn't say so without explaining how I knew. "Have you found his body?"

Jacques shook his head, "No and we won't. According to one of the lackeys he was killed, his body weighted and taken far out to sea where it was dumped overboard."

I shuddered in revulsion. "Was it Perret who killed him?"

"As yet we don't know. Perret is not talking but I suspect it was he who gave the order for both murderers even if he did not strike an actual physical blow."

"He frightens me considerably," I said. "There is something almost inhuman about him."

"This has been a very cleverly orchestrated fraud," my aunt said. "With Castille owning property throughout the country, am I correct in assuming similar thefts are happening elsewhere?"

"Indeed that is correct. It appears what took place here is just the tip of the iceberg, but with our new knowledge thanks to you all, Interpol are as we speak closing in on the rest of the gang in this part of the country and putting an end to the crimes.

"I also arrested Louis Castille last night and have spoken to him in depth regarding his role. His sister remains at their uncle's villa under police guard. At present I am unsure as to the depth of her involvement, but she is fragile and under great stress so I prefer not to throw her in a cell at this stage."

"So how did it all work exactly? I know little bits of course, particularly the parts we all played, but not the larger picture. Perhaps you could explain from the beginning. When did it all start?" my mother asked.

And so Jacques told us what he knew from the beginning.

It all started with Armand Castille's employment of his nephew Louis. He had been given the position of obtaining new business for the art and antiques enterprise, but a playboy at heart and with little business acumen Louis was floundering. He needed desperately to impress his uncle for if he did not he would be dismissed. It was not long after his employment he was arrested.

"By Perret I assume?" I said.

Jacques nodded. "Yes. But what Louis did not know was it had been deliberately manufactured from the start. The boy is completely naive and therefore a prime target for a man with no scruples."

"Or morals or conscience," I added.

Perret apparently had already been involved in some small-time thefts but was looking to move on to bigger things. As a policeman he was in a prime position to divert any inquiry away from the real thieves, and in some cases bury the evidence completely. He had earmarked the Castille art business as a possible place through which he could move stolen artwork but needed someone on the inside. Once Louis had taken a position with the company, Perret used him and continued to apply pressure and blackmail through trumped-up charges. One of his gang had befriended the boy and got him into serious trouble, and then Perret approached, offering to quash the charges provided Louis would work for him. It was expertly done and fear of both his uncle's wrath and the thought of gaol ensured his compliance.

"But surely his uncle would know what was happening in his own business?" my aunt said.

"Eventually he did," said Jacques. "But not for some time. You must remember Armand Castille's business is vast and consists of many companies. The art and antiques was but a small part and more of a hobby; he felt quite safe giving a position to his nephew. However, according to one of Perret's men, Armand discovered the fraud a few months ago and approached his nephew in anger, vowing to go straight to the authorities at the highest level and put an end to it. This of course signed his death warrant for Louis told Perret."

"So we know highly valuable art was stolen from private collections throughout the country, but what happened next?" mother asked.

From an idea supplied to Louis by Perret the art was stolen

and moved to Castille's. Here during the nighttime shift they were protected and covered with blank canvases by a team of dubious but highly skilled and highly paid workers. From there they were 'donated' to the various amateur art schools, such as the one my mother attended, and were painted over by the students who wished for them to be sent on to relatives in their own countries. They passed through the postal services and then were 'stolen' again en-route, where they were matched up with unscrupulous private buyers, who had already paid vast sums of money for the privilege of owning such master artwork, and were never seen again.

"Monsieur Valin was in charge of this aspect, yes?" said Pierre. "But there must also have been someone within the postal service for this to work."

Jacques sighed. "Yes I am sad to say you are correct, Monsieur DuPont. Perret's insidious tentacles are far-reaching; it will take a long time to track down all those involved, if we ever do, and to find the stolen works of art."

"I don't understand why that dreadful display at Tuel's art gallery was necessary," my aunt said, taking my mother's hand and squeezing it in support.

"According to Louis it was twofold," said Jacques. "The first was to shock and intimidate Valin, who as you know had threatened to leave after his argument with Madame Dubois. It's possible also that she had become suspicious of Valin."

"And the second reason?" I said, although I believed I knew the answer.

"To stop you from investigating further. Louis had been told to attend the gallery affair to keep an eye on you. Perret had discovered you were here looking into the colonel's disappearance, and you had connections to Scotland Yard. He wanted an eye kept on you in case you got too close to the truth, and if you had he would have intervened."

"I suppose the weasel told him?"

"Weasel?" Jacques asked, momentarily confused. "Ah, you mean, Belett. Yes he had already told me of your conversation with your colleague Baxter as you know, but he also later informed Perret."

"Is this Belett part of the gang, Captain?" Aunt Margaret asked.

"No, but Perret was his superior officer and he reported back as requested. Perret in return gave him the odd bottle of brandy, good cigars and other gifts in the guise of a friend, but what he was really doing was keeping him onside. Belett is a fool and easily corruptible in a minor way but this level of fraud is way above his head."

"So what did the colonel discover that resulted in his abduction? Did they know he was an undercover British Interpol agent?"

"I don't believe they did at first. I'll tell you what I've been told."

The interviews with those members of the gang Jacques had spoken to had all given their side of the story, and piecing it together he had ascertained that Perret and a couple of his henchmen had followed the colonel to Nice, having become suspicious of him. Upon leaving the train station the colonel's first stop was at his bank where he dropped something in his safety deposit box. From there he had taken lunch at one of the finer hotels, then proceeded to the telephone in the foyer. Masquerading as a customer one of the men had eavesdropped on the conversation, and immediately reported back to Perret that the colonel had said he was close to finding the truth of the art thefts, and he had photographic proof of some high-level police involvement. Perret surmised this was what had been deposited at the bank and immediately gave orders for the colonel to be kidnapped.

"Sometime later your second telephone conversation with Baxter was overheard," Jacques said to me. "Which is when they realised he was an Interpol Agent."

"Did Perret obtain the photographs?" Pierre asked.

"Thankfully no, he probably thought with the colonel out of action they were safer there for the time being. However they have been retrieved today and are every bit as damning as the colonel suggested."

"So you have proof now?"

"We already had proof, Madame Bridges. Thanks to your daughter's bravery last night we overheard Perret's admissions of guilt. The photographs are however an additional nail in his coffin. Now," said Jacques, leaning back and sipping his tea, "I have told you all I know so perhaps you can tell me your side of the story from when I left for Lyon?"

※

So we started with the accident which damaged the painting and Pierre's subsequent discovery of the old master beneath, moving on to his idea of forging the colonel's and returning all three to the art school. Jacques gave me an amused look at the invention of Miss Brown but frowned when he realised we had gone to Castille's with me in disguise.

"That could have been very dangerous," he said.

"My dear Captain Robillard," said Pierre. "We were perfectly safe and besides we learned a great deal."

"And we kept you updated via Beecher. We had no one else we could trust," I said.

Jacques sighed as he realised he was outnumbered but I felt sure I hadn't heard the last of it.

I continued the story with Jacques both nodding and frowning at intervals.

"So," I concluded, "with a good map of the grounds Pierre and myself, along with Gaston, ventured forth last evening to rescue the colonel. The rest you know." I turned to Aunt Margaret and my mother. "So what happened after you left us to take my note to Beecher?"

My aunt took up the narration and explained upon reaching the villa and informing Beecher of the plan he took it upon himself to help. Jacques had not yet returned from Lyon although he was expected back imminently and as luck would have it, he had arrived just as they were leaving.

"So naturally we stayed and brought the captain up to date and he agreed the plan was exceptionally good."

I saw from the corner of my eye Jacques open his mouth to protest, but then thought better of it, and I stifled a giggle. In a short space of time he had already realised he would likely never get the better of my aunt.

"So what exactly was the plan?" I asked. "And where on earth did your costumes come from?"

"Well," said Aunt Margaret. "When Pierre and I went into town to find a suitable costume for you, Ella, alongside the wonderful 'Miss Brown' were three hag costumes. The village players are doing Macbeth this year and I thought they would be perfect so naturally had bought them. It was pure coincidence they were there waiting for Elspeth and I to make use of them last night."

"We all know your penchant for disguise, Maggie," Pierre said, playing with fire. "But why the need last night?"

Aunt Margaret explained it wasn't until they had been informed of the message Gaston had brought from Pierre that the need even arose. However it became apparent that in order to catch Perret and his gang they needed to get inside the compound without raising suspicion, but the entrance was secure and manned by a guard.

"We needed Perret to incriminate himself while we were within hearing distance," Jacques said. "But also to surround them to prevent escape. Gaston, alongside his brothers and Beecher, were to listen at the other side of the wall and go over at the signal. I and my men would creep as close as we could without being spotted and surround them at the other side. My counterpart at the Nice station would stay outside the gates and come to our aid at the first sign of trouble."

"So what was the role of the hags?" I asked.

"To get us through the gate and overcome the guard," mother said. "It was terribly easy too. We would have sneaked in after Perret had entered but the guard closed the gate while in conversation with him, so that wasn't possible. But we had another plan."

Apparently, shortly after they had seen Perret enter, they had turned up at the gates armed with a basket of victuals, mother professing to be the grandmother of one of the guards. Concerned that he was not eating properly she had decided to bring his supper to him, accompanied by her sister who was dumb and a bit addled due to being dropped on her head as a baby.

"I had to think of something on the spur of the moment because Margaret doesn't speak French."

I looked at my aunt who was frowning, this was obviously news to her, and burst out laughing. "Sorry. Carry on," I said, trying to ignore Pierre whose shoulders were shaking with mirth. Even Jacques had a huge grin on his face.

With very little cajoling and promises of a bottle of excellent beer the guard opened the gate and let them in. The beer had been doctored with a sedative beforehand and within minutes he was passed out and snoring in his little hut, while my aunt had taken his keys and unlocked the gates, letting in Jacques and his men.

"And that's all there was to it," mother said. "Now I do believe it's time for tea."

※

"There is just one other thing," Jacques said. "I have had the three paintings you returned examined, and it appears the two remaining masters, the Raphael's, which are supposed to be beneath them are in fact missing."

My mother and I exclaimed in surprise. "But that can't be possible," I said glancing at Pierre. To my astonishment he gave a rather sheepish grin and my aunt sighed. I frowned at them. "Where are they, Pierre?"

"They are still here, in the small room beyond the library."

"So they never left the villa? But why?"

"Because they are some of the most important works of the last centuries. How could we risk them disappearing, never to be found again?"

"Did you know about this, Aunt Margaret?"

"Not at the time, dear, no. Pierre informed me of what he had done while you were at the art school. Had I realised beforehand I would not have agreed. However, by then it was too late."

"You could have told me when we returned."

"I could but then your mind would have been filled with worry rather than concentrating on what you needed to do. Believe me, Ella, I would have told you and Elspeth if I had thought it would achieve anything."

I glowered at Pierre. I was furious that he had risked our lives in such a way and shuddered to think what would have happened to us if Perret had found out about the subterfuge. As though he could read my mind Pierre said, "There was only a small risk, Ella. The forgery was perfect and there was no reason to believe the gang would check the authenticity. They didn't know we had found the masters. They would wish to move them on as quickly as possible. I would not have put your life at risk, you must know that."

I sighed, and then capitulated. "Yes all right, I believe you. Just don't do it again."

"During our next adventure bringing international

thieves, madmen and vagabonds to justice, do you mean?"

I laughed. "I hope I never have to do this sort of thing again. I'm much better at a cerebral approach to investigations as opposed to the physical."

"Oh I don't know, darling, your disguises were excellent. You really are a natural in that regard," said my aunt.

I conceded that that sort of thing may prove useful in the future and was rather fun, but I put my foot down at jumping from the top of cars and walls. "And certainly no more gunfights!"

After tea Jacques asked if I would like to accompany him on a walk along the cliffs. Moving down through the garden we turned right once through the gate, a direction I had not been before, and we hadn't gone far when I recognised a figure sitting on a low wall staring out to sea. As we approached he turned and I recognised Armand Castille come to say goodbye. Standing and giving me a small bow he faded slowly then disappeared completely.

Jacques and I walked in companionable silence for a while enjoying the fresh air and the view.

"I would like to thank you, Ella, for solving this case."

"I didn't do it alone, Jacques. I doubt I would have been able to without the aid of my family."

"Yes of course your family. They are..."

"Odd?" I said.

He laughed. "I was going to say unusual. You all have

unique attributes and experiences as individuals, but put together as a team it is quite formidable."

"Does this mean you are no longer angry about the disguises?"

"I was never angry, Ella. It came from worry for your safety. I would not like anything to happen to you, not now that I have found you."

I blinked in astonishment. Whatever could he mean by that? But he continued to walk as though he had said nothing of import and I put it down to a quirk of translation.

"So what happens next?" I asked.

"I will need to take formal statements from you all over the next few days, and then the investigation will be handed over to Interpol."

"I presumed as much. Were their agents there last night?"

"Yes, although purely in a supportive role. They were happy for me to take the lead."

"And what will happen to Perret?"

"He will hang eventually but there is much we do not know and he is the only one with the answers. He will therefore be housed in a secure and solitary environment while he is interrogated. He will of course be handed over to Interpol."

"So your involvement is almost finished?"

He indicated a bench overlooking the sea and a small cove and we sat in the balmy evening air.

"Actually I have been offered a job with Interpol. This case and the tying up of all the loose ends could take years and I have intimate knowledge."

"Are you going to take it?"

"It would mean spending much time in London. How would you feel about that?"

"Me? Well I think it would be a lovely idea. I live not far from London you know and..." I glanced at his face and saw the amusement tinged with something more raw, and suddenly felt my heart begin to race. He took my hand and gently held it in his.

"In that case I think I will accept."

We sat like that for some time, contented and happy underneath which was a frisson of excitement, and I wondered what my future would hold. But whatever was to happen I could guarantee before very long there would be another mystery to solve.

And as though to reinforce the idea; a black cat with a purple collar and a silver bell silently jumped upon the bench and sat beside me, green eyes staring out into the distance as though he could see the future. And knowing Phantom, he probably could.

Other books in the series:

FREE Prequel Book 0 — The Yellow Cottage Mystery

Find out how it all began…

One glimpse was all it took for a child to fall in love with The Yellow Cottage. Years later she returns as an adult to find it's for sale. But not everything is as it seems…

Will she be able to make this the home she's dreamed about for so long, or will the cottage reject her as it has all others before?

The Yellow Cottage Mystery is the short story prequel to the mystery series and tells the tale of how Ella comes to find the cottage and the adoption of her unusual sidekick.

* *This book is available exclusively to those who sign up to become part of my Reader's Group mailing list. I only send emails to let you know of new releases and never send spam.*

Book One — An Accidental Murder

When a strange child follows her home on the train from London, Ella Bridges feels bound to help her. However she soon discovers the child is not what she seems.

Having recently moved into a large home on Linhay Island, affectionately known locally as The Yellow Cottage, Ella finds herself at the centre of a murder investigation thanks to a special gift from the previous house owner.

Along with her unusual sidekick, a former cottage resident, Ella follows clues which take her to the heart of London.

As the mystery unravels she is forced to enter the lion's den to solve the crime and stop the perpetrator. But can she do it before she becomes the next victim?

Book Two — The Curse of Arundel Hall

One ghost, one murder, one hundred years apart. But are they connected?

Ella has discovered a secret room in The Yellow Cottage, but with it comes a ghost. Who was she? And how did she die? Ella needs to find the answers before either of them can find peace. But suddenly things take a nasty turn for the worse.

Ella Bridges has been living on Linhay Island for several months but still hasn't discovered the identity of her ghostly guest. Deciding to research the history of her cottage for clues she finds it is connected to Arundel Hall, the large Manor House on the bluff, and when an invitation to dinner arrives realises it is the perfect opportunity to discover more.

However the evening takes a shocking turn when one of their party is murdered. Is The Curse of Arundel Hall once again rearing its ugly head, or is there a simpler explanation?

Ella suddenly finds herself involved in two mysteries at once, and again joins forces with Scotland Yard's Police Commissioner to try and catch a killer. But will they succeed?

Book Three– A Clerical Error

When the crime scene is pure coincidence and there's no evidence, how do you prove it was murder?

Ella Bridges faces her most challenging investigation so far when the vicar dies suddenly at the May Day Fete. But with evidence scarce and her personal life unravelling in ways she could never have imagined, she misses vital clues in the investigation.

Working alongside Sergeant Baxter of Scotland Yard, will Ella manage to unearth the clues needed to catch the killer before another life is lost? Or will personal shock cloud her mind and result in another tragedy?

A word about reviews:

Reviews are very important for the success of a book. If you've read and enjoyed any of mine, please leave a review, even if it's just a few words, it really helps. Thank you!

About the Author

J. New has had a lifelong love affair with storytelling in all its forms, so it was only natural that when the opportunity presented itself she would turn to writing books.

Adopted at six weeks old into a loving family, she grew up in a small, picturesque town in West Yorkshire surrounded by nature and with the river Wharfe on her doorstep. Books became her salvation when she found she could 'switch off real life' by immersing herself in the stories, *"I spent a good deal of time either in my own imagination or in someone else's."*

Her choice of genre, British mysteries set in the 1930's, stems from a love of books and films from the era, but the more contemporary ghostly twist originates from personal and family experience.

When not writing she spends her free time with her soul-mate, partner and best friend, (luckily they are all the same person), her rescue animals, gardening, drawing or decorating. A vegetarian, she's also an advocate for holistic, natural health products.

You can connect with her on social media at the following places:

BOOKBUB

https://www.bookbub.com/authors/j-new

FACEBOOK

https://www.facebook.com/jnewwrites

TWITTER

https://twitter.com/newwrites

GOODREADS

http://www.goodreads.com/author/show/7984711.J_New

WEBSITE

https://www.jnewwrites.com/

Printed in Great Britain
by Amazon